Raised in an army family, Ridhi Sarda is an Indian television writer and has worked on television shows like *Khwaabon Ki Zameen Par* and *TV Ke Uss Paar*. Reading is her hobby and she was one of the youngest editors of her school magazine. As a student, she served as jury in two ICYP (International Children and Young People) Film Festivals. She is a marine life enthusiast and writing is her passion. She has also had the privilege to co-author a book on Indian Films with the acclaimed screenwriter Gajra Kottary. This is her first solo attempt at a non-fiction book.

THE MEN WHO DARED

12 Inspiring LIFE stories

RIDHI SARDA

Om Books International

First published in 2024 by

Om Books International

Corporate & Editorial Office
A-12, Sector 64, Noida 201 301
Uttar Pradesh, India
Phone: +91 120 477 4100
Email: editorial@ombooks.com
Website: www.ombooksinternational.com

Sales Office
107, Ansari Road, Darya Ganj
New Delhi 110 002, India
Phone: +91 11 4000 9000
Email: sales@ombooks.com
Website: www.ombooks.com

ISBN: 978-93-5376-888-1

Printed in India

10 9 8 7 6 5 4 3 2 1

For Ahaan. Be the maverick!

CONTENTS

Author's Note

1. SAM MANEKSHAW: The Man Death Feared 1
2. K. K. MUHAMMED: The Temple Warrior 13
3. SUNIL CHHETRI: Uniting India, Playfully! 31
4. SARDAR VALLABHBHAI PATEL: Forging a Nation Out of Chaos 41
5. JADAV PAYENG: The Lone Ranger 57
6. PRINCE MANVENDRA SINGH GOHIL: Only Love Prevails 77
7. MAJOR SANDEEP UNNIKRISHNAN: Duty before Self 93
8. PANDIT BHIMSEN JOSHI: The Voice of God 103
9. PARDEEP SINGH NAGRA: Stay Winning 123
10. SUBHAS CHANDRA BOSE: Faith and Freedom 133

11. CHEWANG NORPHEL: The Ice Man 147

12. SANJIT ROY: Lighting a Revolution 161

Acknowledgements 179

Bibliography 181

AUTHOR'S NOTE

Over the years, it has been real fun to hear my children make declarations about what they wish to be when they grow up. From, "Can I please be a *Doodhwala* because he has the coolest bike and a horn to match?" to a professional pilot, football player, race car driver and even the adorable claim, "When I grow up, I want to be happy!"

The ability of children to believe in themselves combined with their innocence is admirable. Seeing their constantly changing plans, I have silently prayed to God that this childish bravery never abandons them. I have hoped that they remain this way, forever true to their inner voice, never afraid of dreaming or failing. The idea of this book originated in my desire to further inspire this spirit. I found the best way of doing that was by narrating real life stories of people who were tremendously brave in taking the steps that made their life as they had envisioned it to be.

The Men Who Dared covers twelve such personalities from backgrounds as diverse as music, army, politics and activism, archeology, boxing and engineering. These men marched to the beat of their own drum, never surrendering to the challenges that came their way. Their conviction is striking. Moreover, to know their story is to appreciate all the ways in which their achievements have impacted society.

I hope these accounts inspire everyone to dream big and break their idea of success out of prescribed definitions.

I hope it reminds you, dear reader, that you too are free to write your own story.

1

SAM MANEKSHAW

The Man Death Feared

"I am not ready for war."

The words, final and firm, reverberated around the room. They were addressed not just to Prime Minister Indira Gandhi but also to the chiefs of the Armed Forces and top government officials.

Mrs Gandhi was unnerved. When Sam Manekshaw spoke, people listened. After all, his was the voice that commanded the Indian Army. And right now, he was saying that he did not wish to go to war. Mrs Gandhi was reeling from what she had heard. Could this really be the man they famously called 'Sam Bahadur'?

Sam was aware that what he had said was going to be met with tremendous resistance, for the stakes were very high. The tension within East Pakistan was on the rise. Mrs Gandhi had famously declared that India would support East Pakistan in its fight for liberation and self-determination. But what Sam had just refused to do was wage a war to free the people, despite the fact that his Prime Minister wanted it. The press in India wanted it even more. Right now, he was saying that everything the nation was expecting him to do could not be done.

But Sam was not scared. He was *bahadur*—brave. Danger was not new to him. Once a part of the Gorkha regiment in the armed forces, he had stared death in the eyes. He had once embraced nine bullets to his stomach as a soldier. Sam had even quipped that if a man says he isn't afraid of death, he is either lying or he is a Gorkha. And he was not going to be afraid now, when he must defend his decision.

Mrs Gandhi collected her thoughts, and once again looked the Army Chief in the eyes. "Are you saying that you do not wish to go to war, Chief?"

"Yes, Madam Prime Minister, that is exactly what I am saying," Sam replied, not budging from his stance.

The year was 1971. Pakistan's civil war was at its height. The conflict was within the country but when millions of Eastern Pakistanis began to flee to take refuge in India, things began to take a turn for the worse.

For people who were attacked by their own, it was natural for the Eastern Pakistani majority to seek asylum in neighbouring India; and the Indian government gladly gave it to them. But when the trickle of refugees turned into a flood, the refugee camps at the Indian border were strained to capacity and still there seemed no end to the inflow. The Indian government asked for assistance from the governments of the world but despite their assurances, there was no action to back up these promises. Mrs Gandhi realized it was in their hands to solve the issue. So in a remarkably bold move, it was decided that it would be more economical to free East Pakistan by going to war than providing shelter to the endless masses entering India.

These were the last words she was expecting to hear. As an answer to her anxieties, Army Chief Sam continued,

"Madam Prime Minister, my job is to fight, fight to win. And that is why I am saying this to you, if we go to war right now, we will lose. There can be no other outcome." Even as he said it, Sam could sense the air of disapproval in the room. He was admitting his helplessness before the top officials of the country. But Sam would have it no other way. He would rather be honest and get maligned for it than mouth a hundred sugar-coated lies.

Not one to give up easily, Mrs Gandhi finally broke her silence. "I request all of you to excuse us please, the Chief and me that is." She had known him for years. If he said something, he had good instincts backing it up. She sat down next to him. When in the face of stress and danger, most people's sense of humour wanes, for Sam it remained intrinsic, a coping mechanism that he resorted to even now. Before she could say something, he asked, "Prime Minister, should I send in my resignation on grounds of health, physical or mental?"

"Sam, I know you have a good reason for refusing this war. I would like to know what that is."

Sam squared his shoulders. "Madam Prime Minister, like I have said earlier, it is my duty to fight to win. And the timing of this war is not conducive to victory. We are already heading towards the end of April, which means that snow on the Himalayan passes is melting. Once the passes open, and we go into war with Pakistan, China will step up to support them and will have easy access to India via the Himalayan passes. Secondly, the monsoon will soon be upon us and when it rains in Eastern Pakistan, it pours. Rivers turned to oceans will make movement of troops not just difficult but impossible. We will be confined to roads, which will greatly reduce our ability to capture strategic posts. The Air Force will not be able to support us either. Besides, since most of the Army tanks are being re-fitted right now, I will not be able to deploy enough of them in the war. A war at this point is a recipe for disaster."

What he had just said strangely comforted the Prime Minister. What she was being told were hard facts even though she may not like them.

She knew this decision would not come without consequence. Over the past few months, West Pakistan was not just suppressing people of East Pakistan; they had begun a genocidal massacre against them, killing all the people of Bengali descent. Millions were forced to run away from their homes, leaving everything behind. The Chief Ministers of Assam, Tripura and Bengal were left helpless with the number of refugees arriving in their states. They had written letters of desperation to Indira Gandhi asking her to intervene and help solve the crises. Now, she would have to ask them to be more patient because she had no doubts in her mind about the abilities of her Chief of Army.

"Very well, Sam. Do what you need to do." The Prime Minister's confidence in him was all Sam needed; he could now proceed to focus solely on what lay ahead of him.

The task was tough. He had to intervene in the internal affairs of another country, free a region and make sure that his own country was not seen as the aggressor. Things would have to go according to plan. And in case they didn't, he had it in him to overcome that. His whole life was a testimony to it…

In the year 1914, Hormusji Manekshaw, a prominent Doctor was making his way to Lahore by train. With him was his wife Heerabai along with four of their children, Fali, Jan, Sila and Sheroo. A fifth child was on the way. Hormusji was travelling to Lahore where his parents lived. He was to set up an independent medical practice there. But destiny had other plans. When the train stopped in Amritsar, Heerabai knew she could not travel any further, the baby was coming.

And that is how Sam Hormusji Framji Jamshedji Manekshaw was born on the 3rd of April in 1914. The fifth child of his parents, he was the reason they made a stopover in Amritsar. And by the time they were in a comfortable position to resume their journey, they didn't want to. The climate of Amritsar suited them perfectly and so Hormusji decided to set up a practice there itself.

When he finished school at the top of his class, he reminded his father of the promise he had made of letting him study medicine in London. Already supporting the education of his two brothers in London, Hormusji had no choice but to refuse Sam. It broke his heart. The year was 1932 when incidentally, Sam read in the newspapers about the Indian Military Academy being set up in Dehradun. They were to conduct a written exam for selecting appropriate candidates. Since his dream of becoming a doctor already seemed to crumble, an annoyed Sam borrowed five hundred rupees from his mother, went to Delhi and sat for the Military exam. The results were declared and out of thousands of candidates who had applied, only fifteen were selected. To his surprise, Sam had finished sixth. And so, it was the Military that chose him and Sam's path was laid out.

Life in the Indian Military Academy continued to be a grueling one. Spread over 1400 acres, it is here that the first batch of India's Military leaders was trained. Sam would wake up early and go through intense physical training, the mere mention of which could exhaust most. He would go through the entire day without a complaint, the Academy proving to be the perfect outlet to his boundless energy.

After leaving the Academy, he saw action in World War II as part of the British Indian Army. He was sent to war with Burma where he and his men defended a strategic bridge over the Sittaung river. They displayed tremendous courage in holding their post and it was here that Sam was shot not once but nine times by a Japanese soldier in the stomach. So grave was his condition that his commanding officer did not think he would live. Moved by his show of valour, the commanding officer, Sir Cowans, took off the Military Cross given to him for bravery, and pinned it on to the chest of a barely conscious Sam.

Sam was wheeled into the hospital a full thirty-six hours after he was shot; his chance of survival was bleak. But he held on, determined to live. The next task was surgery so that the bullets from his chest and stomach could be removed. But one look at his condition was enough to make most doctors refuse to even touch him.

Finally, his orderly Sher Singh managed to convince an Australian doctor to operate on Sam. The doctor was hesitant since Sam did not seem to be in a good state but he was fully conscious by now. Trying to make him comfortable, the doctor asked Sam what had happened to him. Maybe death was around the corner, but that was never going to change who he was. To make light of the matter, Sam replied, "A bloody mule kicked me."

There, in the makeshift hospital in the middle of war, in front of a fatally wounded Sam, the Australian doctor burst out laughing. He realised that the soldier lying before him had something special in him. The next thing he knew, Sam was moved to a stretcher, getting wheeled in for surgery. The operation was a success and Sam knew that the blessings of his loved ones were with him as he spent his days recovering.

In the year 1947, the British gave up their right to rule on the Indian subcontinent and left. But not before they had broken the nation into two—India and Pakistan. Sam was one of the best officers that both the nations wanted in their armies. He was offered the highest post in the Pakistani Army by the President but he refused as he knew his heart was with India. And so it was here that he stayed.

In the new nation, Sam joined one of the most fearless fighting forces in the world—the Gorkha Rifles, warriors known for never backing off and never accepting defeat even in the face of death. The Gorkhas have been a part of every major Indian war since the nation was formed, clinching victory in the most demanding conditions. Sam was their first non-British officer and he did justice to his rank as their leader. Sam always led by example. He never held anyone up to standards that he himself could not live up to. The Gorkha's were honed into an even more effective fighting force under his leadership and the tales of his bravery were many.

While he was in the Gorkha Rifles, Sam got a name he loved so much that it stuck with him for life. And like most wonderful things, this too happened to him by accident. While passing him by, Sam happened to ask a soldier what his name was. *"Tera naam kecho?"* Sam said. Without missing a beat, the guard replied, "Harka Bahadur, Guru." As an afterthought, Sam asked him if he knew what his name was. "*Mera naam kecho?*" Quick as lightning, the soldier replied, "Sam Bahadur."

As fate would have it, from that day onwards, he became Sam Bahadur or Sam the Brave. A title he wholly lived up to all his life.

In the year 1962, there was an unexpected attack on India by China. While India's decision to give asylum to the Dalai Lama fuelled the fire, the primary reason for the attack was a piece of land lying along the Himalayan border. India was not prepared for a war. The field of clash was the harsh mountainous terrain making it a difficult task to wage war. At this time, Prime Minister Jawaharlal Nehru trusted Sam to take over the command. Not one to back down from a challenge and always ready to defend the country, Sam took charge and with the help of the Air Force, tried to contain a war that had spiraled out of control. For his efforts, Sam was appointed the Chief of Army Staff in the year 1969.

And now, Nehru's daughter was in charge and he was ordered to go to war against Pakistan. Sam knew there was no room to make mistakes. The country was waiting. The world was watching. If he failed, it would be a major humiliation for the nation. Sam spent the next few months in making battle plans, strengthening the morale of the Army and ensuring that the military equipment was faultless. No detail was too small for his attention. He knew he had a great responsibility on his shoulders, and he was going to ensure he justified the trust that was placed in him.

He did not have to wait long. Early December that year, India was pulled into the war when Pakistan made aerial strikes on eleven Indian Air Force stations. India was now the victim of aggression, and it had the right to fight back. And so, on the 4th of December, the Indian Army attacked the Pakistani Army present in East Pakistan. This was the point when India entered the war, supporting East Pakistan and the Bengali nationalist forces.

The Indian soldiers fought bravely and honorably, ensuring safe passage for women, children and the elderly. And Sam was monitoring it every step of the way from Delhi. Every morning at 8:30, Sam would meet Prime Minister Indira Gandhi to brief her on the developments of the war.

While the world watched and did nothing to stop the atrocities against human rights in East Pakistan, India went ahead and sent her soldiers to their defense. With an excellent Commander-in-chief who believed victory was imminent, thirteen days after the war began, India had achieved a clear advantage over the West Pakistani forces. On the 16th of December, Pakistani military signed the instrument of surrender in Dhaka. It was this city that was made the capital of the new free country that is marked on the map as Bangladesh.

A triumphant Mrs Gandhi congratulated Sam and gave him credit for this win. But Sam himself had no time to exalt in this success. A war often left behind many casualties. The soldiers fighting on the Indian side had to be brought back home, the martyrs had to be given an honorable send off, their families had to be taken care of and there was the matter of the Pakistani soldiers who had been captured. A total of ninety-three thousand Pakistani soldiers had been taken prisoners by the Indian Army after the war had ended.

Sam had given standing orders to the Army that these prisoners of war were to be treated with respect. Once in India, they were placed in jails but given the respect that befitted a soldier. A lot of Pakistani prisoners were surprised when he went into their cells and prison barracks on a surprise check. He enquired after their well-being, if mosquitoes or bed bugs bothered them. He tasted the food they were being given to check its quality and was even concerned for their hygiene and health.

Eventually, all the prisoners of war were released and sent back. After the Indo-Pak war, Sam went on an official visit to Pakistan. One evening, when he was at a state dinner at the residence of the Governor of Pakistan, he received a rather unusual request. The Governor told Sam that some soldiers wished to see him. As Sam made his way to see the soldiers, he was surprised to see all of them standing in formation. They saluted him and then, in an act of tremendous respect, placed their turbans at his feet. Astonished, Sam wanted to know the reason behind this gesture. One of the men then came forward and told him how all five of his sons had been prisoners in the Indo-Pak war. They all came back safe and sang tales of how they were treated with dignity in India. So many families did not lose their sons because of Sam and they were grateful to him. And Sam was grateful to their show of gratitude.

In 1973, Sam was given the title of 'Field Marshal' by the prime minister. A few weeks later, Sam retired from the

Indian Army, after having served the nation for forty long years. He spent the rest of his life in Coonoor pursuing his hobbies of fishing and photography. The soldier could finally rest, knowing he had done well to serve his country.

2

K. K. MUHAMMED

The Temple Warrior

It was a hot and dry afternoon in the sparsely populated village of Bateshwar. Muhammed was looking at what was once a beautifully constructed temple, but now was not more than a frame of stones worn with time. The temple was made between the 9th and the 11th century. He could see the etchings of Ganesha at the centre of the frame, of what may have once been the entrance to the temple. But Muhammed had no clue which deity may have resided within.

Muhammed forced himself to forget about the magnitude of what he had undertaken to do and focus on taking just one step ahead. In the moment, he felt like circling the temple and he knew better than to dismiss such instincts. It was through these instincts that he had felt the earth speak to him. Like when she had guided him about the location of Mughal Emperor Akbar's Ibadat Khana. She never let him down and often led him in the right direction. It was through this faith that Muhammed had learnt to dream big.

Desperate for a clue, Muhammed began to walk around the temple in a *parikrama*. He looked at the rectangular shaped hole that lay right before the entrance to the temple. Had the hole been square in shape, it may have been the place where the Garuda Stambh or pillar is usually erected in a temple dedicated to Vishnu. But there are no construction plans available for temples built between the 9th and 11th century!

But then, where was Nandi? Worshipped as the animal form of Shiva, Nandi is his beloved devotee. Where there is Shiva, there is Nandi. Muhammed looked around but he could not spot the statue of the rightful occupant of the gaping rectangular hole.

As he walked, he reflected on the path he had set out on. It was not a simple one. As an archaeologist, the task he had undertaken was terribly daunting to say the least. It was the reason that he was standing here in the ruins of about two hundred temples spread over a vast area, the only place of its kind in the world.

Soft spoken and humble, the fifty-one-year-old Muhammed was born to Beeran Kutty Haji and Mariyam in the village of Koduvally in Kerela. Life was hard for the family; with the parents' lack of education and their lack of money. Yet his father's dedication to provide him and his four siblings a decent education proved fruitful.

After finishing his school in Koduvally, he did a master's in history from Aligarh Muslim University. It was his love for history that prompted him to get a post-graduate diploma in archaeology from the Archaeological Survey of India, New Delhi. From there began a career that would take Muhammed places he had never imagined, making discoveries that would stun the world. Among his many notable projects was the discovery of Akbar's Ibadat Khana, excavations of Ram

Mandir, restoration of the Dantewada temples, and the excavation of the Stupa of Kesaria built by Emperor Ashoka. It was his passion that conceived and executed the idea of building a museum that exhibits replicas of historical Indian statues and sculptures. The Replica Museum currently stands outside Siri Fort Sports Complex in New Delhi.

Through it all, he continued working towards helping people, especially young children. From his father, a humble man deeply connected to his roots, Muhammed had inherited the value of giving back. He had often seen his father help those who were in need, despite the difficulties that they faced. And when Beeran Kutty's financial position improved, he would feed about a hundred children every year in the month of Rabi-ul-Awwal, the third month of the Islamic calendar corresponding to the beginning of spring. For his part, when Muhammed worked on the conservation and restoration of monuments in Delhi, he ran at least five schools for the children of the migrant workers who were engaged on these sites. It was not uncommon for Muhammed to give them food and uniforms for free and to help them secure permanent jobs with the government. He did this to emulate his father and walk in his steps

Muhammed's love for history and his scholarship in Sanskrit was to lead him to the most challenging and rewarding project of his career—the restoration of more than a hundred breathtakingly beautiful temples, over one thousand three hundred years old, that lay crumbled like Lego pieces in Bateshwar.

In the year 2003, Muhammed was posted at Gwalior in Madhya Pradesh. Always eager to make a difference wherever he worked, Muhammed wanted the most challenging site to be his project. Little did he know his wish was to come true in the form of the Bateshwar Temple Complex that lay about forty kilometres from Gwalior, a cluster of about two hundred temples and shrines.

Bateshwar immediately had Muhammed's attention. But the more he probed, the more he was discouraged from pursuing the task. The biggest reason to which was, Bateshwar being located in the depths of the Chambal valley, an area overrun by gangs of dacoits. Muhammed was told that working at Bateshwar meant first negotiating with the dacoits and then with the mining mafia, which was nothing but inviting trouble. Several Police Officers had been kidnapped and even murdered in Chambal. Entire police parties were trapped and attacked often. Dacoits with huge rewards on their heads and murder on their hands, roamed free here.

Armed gangs of robbers have been roaming the lands of India since the thirteenth century. However, they gained notoriety during the British Raj. Feared for attacking businessmen and travellers, the dacoits often operated on Robin Hood principles—keeping a portion of the loot for themselves and distributing the rest among the poor. Gradually they surrendered or were shot dead.

In 2004, there were several notorious dacoits that had the free run of Chambal. All of them were extremely reluctant to give up their territory. There was Man Singh, a dacoit charged with 1,112 robberies and 185 murders including 32 police officers. Malkhan Singh was charged for a 100 murders. So widespread was his fear among people that when he wanted a ransom, he would send a letter to the victim's family on his letterhead. Then there was Paan Singh Tomar, a retired Army man who had represented India in the Olympics.

But one of the most fearsome of the dacoits was Nirbhay Singh Gujjar, known as the Lion of Chambal as he controlled the whole area. He ran a parallel government of his own in about forty villages. In the thirty-years of his dominion, there were a total of 239 criminal cases filed against him for murder, robbery and kidnapping. Negotiating with him was next to impossible. Going to Bateshwar without Nirbhay's permission meant risking death. It was rumored that even the animals around those ruins feared him. An air of mystery surrounding the ruins made anyone who wanted to even wander there think twice.

Yet Muhammad insisted on working there! One of his staff members even warned him that murder and kidnapping would be par for the course for anyone who wanted to even interact with Nirbhay. But he could feel a pull towards Bateshwar that he could not put into words. Mother earth was calling him; a lot of work was to be done. Muhammad was not going to chicken out now. And so, despite the protests from his peers, seniors and juniors, Muhammed knew he would take up the Bateshwar restoration project. To all the naysayers, he had just one answer—he would do it anyway. If they helped him, together they would make far more progress. In the face of such determination, the ASI team soon made a breakthrough in the form of Special Director General CRPF (Central Reserve Police Force) Vijay Raman.

Muhammed could work at the Bateshwar Temple Complex with protection from the police. General Raman gave many helpful tips to Muhammed like never sharing the details of his trip with too many people or taking the same route twice.

But even with the police backing them, Muhammed knew if he had the support of the dacoits, he could go much further. This was not an assignment where he could just go and fix a place. This was an assignment that would need the co-operation of all the stakeholders, a project that would need social engineering. He would have to make even the dacoits feel like they had a part to play in bringing back to life the work of their ancestors.

An unusual request was made of General Raman. It was this request that was playing on his mind when Muhammed set out to go to his office one Sunday. "Are you going to the office today?" asked his wife Rabiya, her brows creased in surprise. He nodded in reply. "But why?" she asked. He was always at work. Sunday should be her time with him. "To have tea with a dacoit," he muttered and left Rabiya wondering the nature of this madness. "But…but that isn't a part of your job…" She struggled to discourage him. "True, maybe it's a perk," replied Muhammed with a glint in his eyes. And before she could say more, he was out the door, leaving her wondering what new trouble was heading their way.

With Raman's help, Muhammed met Lacchu Singh. While this was a new experience for Muhammed, he knew he had to go through it. The meeting proved to be a breakthrough and helped Muhammed gain the dacoits' approval. Soon even more dacoits that had surrendered came up to assist Muhammed in the task.

And then came the day Muhammad had been waiting for. Muhammed's team had been trying to establish contact with

Nirbhay Singh's gang for a long time. Finally, word came from the other side.

He was at work when Muhammed noticed the worried looks of his co-workers. "What is it, why do all of you look so worried today?" he asked them as they cast furtive glances at him. One of his juniors stepped up to answer, "Sir, a message has arrived for you through one of the surrendered dacoits. It is from Nirbhay Singh. He wants to know why our team would want to restore temples deep in the jungle, where no one ever comes." This was a good sign. The dacoit was willing to talk. On his part, Muhammed sent an honest answer, leaving no room for confusion. "Please tell him that the site, like all other lands in the country, is the property of the Government of India. And it is the wish of the government that the temples be restored."

"Hmmm..." said Nirbhay Singh when the reply was faithfully repeated to him by one of his men. He took one long puff of the *beedi* he was smoking and looked around him. "For anyone to want to fix this place, he would have to be mad. It is impossible." He had half a mind to say no. And with his influence, he could afford to say no even to the Indian Government. After all, more than forty villages were under his control. He stood up and began to walk around, his trusted gun in one hand, *beedi* in the other. He was thinking about this most unusual request he had received. He wondered if this officer really had it in him.

Muhammed was having his breakfast when the second message from Nirbhay Singh came. This time his subordinate looked worried. Not one to waste time in unnecessary speculation, Muhammed asked him to just say it like it is. "Sir he has one more question—Why is the team to restore temples being headed by a Muslim? And that too by one called Muhammed. He says even Ghazni and Ghori, conquerors who destroyed our temples, were called Muhammed." A smile came to Muhammed's lips. He had his answer ready.

Muhammed's words were carefully relayed to Nirbhay. He had said, "Their name is the only thing I share. Like this is your motherland, it is mine too. Not everyone wishes to destroy. Let me show you." The answer was crisp and to the point. Nirbhay was intrigued. He had heard a lot of empty promises in his life. It would be interesting to see if this was one of them. "I give him four months to fix the entrance of this place. Let's see if he can work as well as he talks."

"Sir, the topography of Chambal is like a maze. It is full of tall dunes made of sand. No one has been able to master this area, but the dacoits know it like the back of their hands. They have made pathways inside the dunes and they know their way in and out of them. So many police officers have lost their lives here, so many have been kidnapped and killed." Muhammed had no time to think about any of this. He had just received word that they had the go-ahead from Nirbhay. That was all that mattered.

Not one to waste time, while the negotiations were going on with Nirbhay Singh, Muhammed had been studying the land of Bateshwar. Several books and maps had helped him gather a fair idea of the place by now. So, when the word finally came from Nirbhay, Muhammed was ready. Armed with his notes, he set out for Bateshwar with his team members and a lot of police officers. Throughout their expedition, not just the staff of the ASI but even the police was looking over their shoulders. To say that their lives depended on the way this assignment progressed would not have been far-fetched. It was the first time worries assailed Muhammed, not so much for himself but for the entire team which was risking their lives to be with him. Hoping for the best, Muhammed moved ahead with a prayer on his lips…

Despite all that he had heard of the ruins of Bateshwar, nothing came close to what he was to witness at the site. About an hour and a half away from Gwalior, in the district of Morena, Bateshwar was in a terrible condition, with not a single structure fully intact. Debris and sand stretched as far as the eye could see, foliage was growing out of some ruins, and no source of water was available for miles. The place was desolate, save for some polythene bags, liquor bottles and the remains of bonfires—a stark reminder that the ASI team was on a land loaned to them even if it belonged to the Government.

Fear reared its ugly head in Muhammed's heart. He was responsible for all the people he had brought here. What if something went wrong? But he realized the only way forward was to not be afraid. He looked at his team members who looked like they could do with some encouragement. "Do you know what a famous travel writer said when he saw a picture of this place? He called it the biggest jigsaw puzzle in the world. Now that's encouraging!" There was soft laughter in the crowd. Muhammed then said, "My friends, if we can see the lighter side of our situation while never forgetting the gravity of the work we have undertaken, we should be fine. Shall we begin then?" Like the roar of lions, his team members responded by shouting, "Yes, sir!" in unison. Their voices echoed in the jungles, heard by more people than their eyes could see.

Since this was holy ground, Muhammed ensured that they got to work only after praying to Lord Shiva. The team of ASI had extensively pored over history books for clues about the type of architecture at Bateshwar. They knew that these temples had been made by the Gurjara-Pratihara dynasty between the 8th and the 11th century. The Gurjaras were Suryavanshis, descendants of the Sun of the lineage of Lakshmana, the brother of Lord Rama.

Eighth to eleventh century was also the time when many other great temples were being made on the land based on this kind of architecture, like the temples at Khajuraho by the Chandela dynasty, Brihadeshwara temple dedicated to Shiva by Rajaraja I of the Chola Empire, and the Konark temple dedicated to the Sun.

While the temples had probably fallen due to a series of earthquakes hundreds of years ago, their two outer frames miraculously survived. Using these as a reference, Muhammed's team established that the temples were made on the Maru-Gurjara style of architecture that was prevalent in the region at that point in time. In this style, the exterior walls of the temple were made of projections and recesses, which had deities in them.

This brought a very interesting detail into focus. Beginning with the feet of the temple—the *Vedibandha* part, the *Jangha* section that lies above the knee, the *Varandika* or the waist section and the head—the *Shikhara*, the temples at Bateshwar had an anatomy of their own, almost like a human being.

Armed with this knowledge, Muhammed and his team now began to make regular trips to Bateshwar. With the immunity given to them by the dacoits and the deadline of four months, they had a lot of work to do.

On one such trip, the team was trying to figure out where the foundation of the entrance lay. They had cleared the area of all the pillars and fallen pieces of the temples. Feeling the eyes of someone watching his back, Muhammed spotted a man sitting outside a temple at a distance. Even though alone, he seemed like someone better left to his own devices. Something told Muhammad that he should stay away.

Unknown to Muhammed, he was being assessed by none other than Nirbhay. Now Muhammed had seen him too. He knew the Muslim temple restorer would not dare approach him. But he was surprised when Muhammad began to walk towards him.

Muhammed did not know who the man dressed in a *dhoti* and *kurta,* with a huge vermilion mark on his forehead, was. His beard and moustache made him look like he was from one of the villages nearby. But what caused Muhammed some consternation was that this man was dropping ash and damaging the priceless stones and relics at the site. He was going up to him to ask him to stop smoking.

Just then, one of his juniors ran to him asking him not to approach the mustachioed man, telling him it was the Lion himself—Nirbhay Singh Gurjar. "Sir, don't go there. Let him be and he will leave on his own in a little while," said the breathless junior. But with this knowledge everything changed. Muhammed had to speak to him now.

Nirbhay Singh watched as the man from the ASI approached him. He continued to smoke his *beedi* as he sat on his haunches. After all, this was his haunt and the ASI the interlopers. He eyed Muhammed nonchalantly. And then Muhammed spoke, "Nirbhay-ji, thank you very much." Of all the things Nirbhay was expecting to hear, this was not it. Muhammed had now made Nirbhay curious. Muhammed continued, "All these priceless idols and artifacts that are lying here are still in India because of you. Otherwise, they would have been stolen long ago and would be sitting today in some auction house in France or America."

The way he said these words made Nirbhay feel they were genuine. He moved slightly, as if indicating that Muhammed could sit near him. It was a significant gesture coming from a man who was not exactly thrilled about having complete strangers have a run of his domain. Muhammed sat down near Nirbhay. He then said, "It is not a coincidence that we have met. Your name is Nirbhay Singh Gurjar. You are a descendant of the Gurjaras who made these temples thousands of years ago. It is, therefore, your duty to protect these temples, is it not?" Muhammed's words had found their mark. Nirbhay put out his *beedi* but there was a difference. This time he was careful not to cause any damage to the stones lying around. And then he got up and walked away.

If Muhammed was surprised, he did not show it. He had far too much on his hands and mind. There was a lot to be done. Special skilled *karigars* or workers were needed to restore the *Garbhagriha* or the sanctum sanctorum of the temples.

Skilled workers were also needed to restore the ceilings. But infested as the place was with dacoits, the workers were unwilling to come to work at this site.

As if in an answer to his prayers, Nirbhay sent a message to Muhammed a few days later that he could bring in all the workers he needed to complete the task. From then on, there was no turning back. Along with the skilled workers, there was also a need to make this project economically viable for the villagers of the surrounding areas, so that even they felt involved. By making them partners, rather than just hire them, meant they would play an active part in conserving the site in the future as well. This social engineering could keep the place intact. But the locals themselves were unaware of the treasure they had. To solve this problem, Muhammed held meetings with the villagers, emphasizing the significance of the temples at Bateshwar.

With a competent workforce in place consisting of skilled *karigars* and sensitized villagers, work on restoring the temples began in full swing. Since pillars, debris and artifacts covered the entire area, the first step was to get the site cleared, and each piece had to be stored properly to avoid any further damage. The team began with locating the foundations of the temples at the entrance of the area, a task made difficult by the weight of each piece that had to be removed. Muhammed and his team worked day and night to locate every piece as per the anatomy of the temple. Once the missing pieces of a temple were located, they would be glued back with lime or *Surkhi* (burnt bricks ground to powder).

Muhammed's task was further complicated by the missing pillar of the entrance. After extensively searching and excavating nearby, they managed to locate not just the other pillar but the base of the pillars as well. Work was finally picking up pace.

With not a single temple intact as their guide, Muhammed and his team worked on their instincts. Some structures that were left standing were so fragile that they could crumble with a mere touch. For such structures, Muhammed and his team would make extensive drawings and take photographs. Then they would dismantle the whole thing and take it apart. All so they could lay a strong foundation for the temple. And then, the entire temple would be reconstructed so that it would withstand the next five hundred years!

Since Muhammed was working on a deadline that was fast approaching, he divided the entire area of the entrance into several sections, putting people in charge of each. It was almost like performing a surgery; even a slight error could have heavy consequences. Time was of essence. Everyone in the team knew that by restoring the entrance of the Bateshwar Temple Complex, they were showing the dacoits the possibilities of their restoration project.

Sooner than they could imagine, four months had come to an end. Rumours began to do the rounds that Nirbhay Singh wanted to see for himself the work they had done. This was the moment of reckoning for the whole team. Hard work never goes in vain. And sure enough, when Nirbhay Singh and his gang came around, they were amazed by the pillars, arches and a few temples standing where there was only rubble before. It was impossible to believe they had achieved such a feat in so short a time. Astonished, Nirbhay Singh called it a *chamatkaar*. The will of one man was enough to make a difference in the world, this Nirbhay knew. After all, he was proof of it.

"You must carry on the good work. And if you need more men, I am willing to give you the help you need," Nirbhay said to Muhammed, a huge victory in itself. There was no looking back now.

Even so, the work of the ASI at Bateshwar was often complicated by unexpected problems. One such instance was when there was a tree growing on a temple. The roots of the tree had penetrated even the foundations of the structure. At such times, Muhammed felt that simply cutting away the tree was wrong. But removing it was also necessary. Muhammed then approached the tree and began to pray to it. He asked for forgiveness from the tree by chanting and begged pardon from all the birds and insects, even going so far as to give them the reason as to why he was forced to cut the tree. Muhammed prayed for the living creatures on the tree to migrate to other trees nearby and only then did he give the permission for it to be cut.

But as soon the tree was cut down, the temple structure crumbled completely. They would have to begin from the very foundations of the temple. To the surprise of the ASI, even the dacoits joined in to help with the restoration work. And they proved to be hard workers. Watching them work so diligently, Muhammed often felt that in a way, along with restoring the temples, the dacoits were rebuilding their own lives too. These were people who had faced cruelty in life and as a result had set out to make the world pay for it. But now they were realizing how God could reside even in total devastation. How could their lives be any different then?

The temples stood tall in the sun. These restored structures were an ode to the workmanship of the people who made them thousands of years ago. Each completed structure was a testament to the power of persistence and a good cause. For Nirbhay Singh, this was the will of God. For Muhammed, this was the will of Shiva for He is the one who eternally remains.

Being so connected to the earth, Muhammed often found her speak to him in unexpected ways. When drinking water was a problem, something told Muhammed that a solution was at hand. Sure enough, they discovered a *Pushkarni* or sweet water well. By tracing the source of its water and clearing up the channels, Bateshwar now had a steady supply of drinking water for the locals and dacoits. This project had greatly benefitted everyone. The place really had the presence of Lord Shiva performing his cosmic dance.

Time had flown and here he was trying to solve another puzzle with Earth as an ally. He was completing the *Parikrama* of the temple with the gaping rectangular hole. He willed the stones to talk to him, to tell him if the temple once belonged to Lord Shiva.

As he neared the back of the temple, he could not believe his eyes. There, amid the rubble of hundreds of temples, slightly apart from the rest, half buried in sand, lay the perfectly carved statue of Nandi, the bull. There it lay, as if it had been waiting to be found for thousands of years, to go back to where it had always belonged. A smile came to his lips, his hands rose in salutation to the Creator. He respectfully picked up the statue, completed the *Parikrama* and walked back to the gaping rectangular hole.

Nandi was finally home!

3

SUNIL CHHETRI

Uniting India, Playfully!

India's fight for Independence had once found a place on the football pitch. In 1911, the English were left red-faced in their colony, when India won the International Football Association finals. It is still remembered as India's clarion call for freedom that reached the sports field.

When the Indian team qualified for FIFA in 1950, the players of an Independent India could not go because the All India Football Federation lacked the means to support it. Yet, the 50s and early 60s proved to be the Golden age of Indian football, owed largely to the player and coach Syed Abdul Rahim. Under his wing, the team became the best in Asia, and sadly, after his death in 1963, India could never play up to that level.

Slowly, a sport that was once loved by the nation was relegated to the sidelines, for another to take centre stage. Cricket rose as a phenomenon, a religion, becoming the most viewed, played, sponsored and supported game in the country. Over the years, despite Indian football giving many excellent players to the field, not enough fans remained to cheer for them. A lot of Indian football fans had shifted their allegiance to European clubs by then—it was no longer as popular among the general public.

Until along came one man who refused to let things stay the way they were. His love for football was infectious. It made the Indian football fans sit up and take note. They were forced to wonder why they had for so long ignored the trove of Indian football talent in favour of players from foreign shores. That man was Sunil Chhetri.

Amidst the packed shelf of Chhetri's shiny trophies and solid medals, one award gleams out conspicuously. It is a wooden cutout of a golden coloured bird that looks suspiciously like the icon of Twitter. It rests as a memento of the one appeal he made to his country and how that changed the course of Indian football.

On June 1st, the Indian National Football Team played the first football match of the Intercontinental Cup 2018 against Chinese Taipei. India was the home team playing at the Mumbai Football Arena. The result was a 5-0 win for India against a very competitive side. Sunil had scored three of those five goals. The Indian team had got off on a fantastic start. But despite all the success, Sunil was disappointed. The reason was his missing family—the spectators! In a stadium capable of hosting thousands, only a little over two thousand people had come to see the match.

Looking at the empty stands, the 5-0 victory of the Indian team seemed like a party that no one turned up for. It broke Sunil's heart. He could have turned a blind eye to it and continued the winning streak of his side as the Captain.

But because he was the Captain, he decided to do something no player had ever done before.

On the 2nd of June, the nation woke up to a video posted on Twitter by Sunil Chhetri. There, sitting in his blue jersey of the Indian National Team, Sunil's cri de coeur was for the nation to hear…

…To everyone who is not a football fan, please come and watch us. Two reasons… Number one: It's the best game in the world. Number two: We play for our country. We'll make sure that once you come to watch us, you will not go the same person back home.

To all of you who are fans of big European clubs and support your European clubs with so much passion. And sometimes you guys think that the level is not the same so why to waste your time... Agreed. The level is not the same. Not even close, but with our desire and determination we'll make sure, we'll try our best to make your time worth.

To all of you who have lost hope or don't have any hope in Indian football, I request you to come and watch us in the stadiums. I mean it's not fun to criticize or abuse on the internet. Come to the stadium, do it on our face. Scream at us, shout at us, abuse us. Who knows one day, one day we might change you guys and you might start cheering for us. Please come...

To all of you who are fans and could not come/ did not come/ delay/ work/ school, please come and watch in the stadiums. Come and watch us in the stadiums. You guys have no idea how important you guys are… how important your support is.

When Chhetri, with folded hands, made this heartfelt plea to the nation he did what no player had ever done before. He put his heart out there before his people. He risked ridicule or worse, complete indifference. But no sooner was his video out it went viral on the internet. It brought people to the stadium at the Mumbai Football Arena in unprecedented numbers for the next match that India was to play, and they all cheered for the Indian team. The atmosphere was electric.

Witnessing the nation's support in their next game against Kenya, the Indian Football Team scored another win going on to win the 2018 Intercontinental Cup. It was a very special win. People had shown their love and support for Sunil and the Indian football team in a big way. It was a gesture that he would never forget. Always working hard, never giving up, and learning from his mistakes to make his game better—that is Sunil Chhetri. Playing for the country is a responsibility he takes very seriously. But then, Sunil has always been that dutiful, be it on or off the pitch.

Chhetri was born in Secunderabad on 3rd August in 1984 to parents of Nepalese origin. Kharga Chhetri was in the Indian Army while Sushila Chhetri was a home-maker. Both of them played football so it wasn't a surprise that Sunil too gravitated towards it. His mother had played in the Nepalese National team before her marriage. As a child, he would spend hours playing ball. His mother would finish off her chores and join him, teaching him a trick here and a move there. Meanwhile his father played football as part of routine in the regiment he was in, participating in several matches. And though he could not fulfil it due to his responsibilities, playing for the Kolkata based Mohun Bagan Football Club, one of Asia's oldest and most prestigious, remained a long cherished dream for Kharga.

With his father in the Army, the family was constantly on the move, from Gangtok to Darjeeling to Kolkata and Delhi. The places kept changing but Sunil's passion for football only grew. Along with it also grew the number of things he ended up breaking at home because of the ball! Every time his unsuspecting mother discovered yet another article in pieces; her only recourse was a spanking for Sunil. And in a routinely fashion, before she could lay her hands on him, Sunil would promptly run away from her sight.

When he wasn't busy escaping his mother's temper, Sunil was busy coercing her to play ball with him. He wasn't choosy about where he got to play. The tiniest of spaces were perfect for him as long as he got to play with his parents and learn. He immensely enjoyed those gaming sessions with his parents. And he learnt from them a very important trait, that of sportsmanship. His parents would ensure he played by the rules, never going soft on him just because he was a child. That taught him to play by the rules and to win fair. Any notions of expecting favours because of his age were forgotten by Sunil even before they could form. So it happened, while growing up, Sunil's biggest competitor remained his mother. He would try to beat her at all kinds of games, including football.

His father, with a young family to support as well as his parents back in Nepal, would often have to be away for work. And Sunil, even as a young child realized quite soon the sacrifices his parents would make to make do with what they had. In Nepal, when a son grows up, his mother begins to call him Bhai, implying that the son is now ready to shoulder the responsibilities of the family. Sushila began to call her son Bhai at a very young age because of the way Sunil made sure he was always there whenever he was needed. Contrarily, he never bothered his parents for anything. Whether it was toys or clothes, he learnt to buy these things for himself with the prize money he got by playing matches of football and cricket. It was a habit he formed early in life. And just as he saw his own father do, Sunil took it upon himself early on to look after his father.

At the time when Sunil was studying in the Army Public School in Delhi, sports shoes defined what it meant to be 'the coolest'. While other kids his age were wearing expensive shoes to school, Sunil never could. Expenses had to be reasonable and measured. So when he got to know about a tournament called the Milo Tournament for Football, he immediately signed up for it. The prize money for the best player was Rs. 1,500, a princely sum at that time.

Sunil participated in it and gave it his all. This was the one thing he had always loved after all. And sure enough, by the end of the Milo tournament, Sunil was named the best player. Any teenager would have been delighted in spending the money he earned on himself. Like all the other kids, Sunil too wanted a nice pair of branded sports shoes. But he could see beyond his wants, and chose to buy two pairs of less expensive shoes with the prize money, one for himself and the other for his father. Despite Kharga's protests, he was gifted new shoes by his young son, a gesture that moved him to tears. It was proof of the upbringing he had received and also a sign of the conscientious young man he was to become.

Sunil played in the Milo tournament for three years and each year, Kharga was gifted a new pair of shoes.What made the father proud beyond words was how caring and responsible Sunil was even at that age. It was a simple act, but it made Sunil realise how happy he was when he could do what he loved and bring joy and pride to somebody else. He began to nurture the dream of playing for his country one day.

When he was in the eleventh standard, he played in the Under 17 tournament in Delhi and with that began his journey to start playing professional football. But to make it big in the world of professional football, Sunil needed a slight push. And that came in the form of a senior from his school. Amit Sharma was a very well-known name in Indian football from the team Hindustan FC. He was considered the best player in Delhi. It was he who noticed when Sunil played, and recommended Sunil for the same club. For a young boy to get spotted and then selected to play for a well-known club was like a dream come true. Grateful for the chance, Sunil put in the extra hours and work to better his game and prove that he was indeed the right choice.

That was his first break. Refusing to let it go in vain, Sunil wanted to make Amit proud. He did well for himself, even getting a chance to play in the preliminary round of the Durand Cup, the oldest football tournament in Asia. And sure enough, he was noticed.

At the preliminary round, Sunil was observed by the members of Mohun Bagan. This was huge since Mohun Bagan is one of Asia's oldest and the most prestigious football clubs in India. The same club that his father had harboured a dream to play for. And the son was on his way to living that dream, when he was invited to Kolkata by the club.

He was under the impression that he was being asked to give a trial for getting admitted into the Mohun Bagan Academy, which alone would have been a matter of prestige. But on reaching Kolkata, he realized he had been given direct admission into the club. The endless hours, days and weeks that he had spent at practice were bearing their fruits. At one of the matches that Sunil played in Delhi, he had executed a flawless bicycle kick known as the *Shyam Thapa bicycle kick*. This master kick is named after the national team football player Shyam Thapa who was a bronze medalist in the 1970 Asian Games. Among the witnesses of that stunt was Subrata Bhattacharya, coach to Mohun Bagan and also a former player.

Joining Mohun Bagan as a full-time player meant the one thing Sunil had wanted the most—a career in football.

Soon the seventeen-year-old was playing for the club and carrying the remnants of his father's dream into reality. Being a young player and an expert at his game, he made a lot of headlines. And while it had its advantages, Sunil also had to go through the grind. He wasn't unaware of the harsh reality of making a career in a sport that wasn't cricket. Passion couldn't alone pay the bills. While the practice sessions proved grueling, they were a cake walk compared to the actual match. Mohun Bagan was worshipped by its fans. This meant that the players were put on a pedestal when they scored but were ripped apart when they failed.

Sunil was often subject to the anger of fans. It unnerved him how quickly the fans could go from loving to ruthlessly criticizing you in minutes. But in that too he found inspiration. It made him realise how the fans were deeply connected to the club; it made him want to perform even better.

After three years of training, playing and learning in Mohun Bagan, it was time to move on. Sunil now joined the JCT Football Club in Punjab. The year was 2005 and Sunil's new coach was Sukhwinder Singh. Here there was a lot more to learn for the young man who had just arrived. He realized he had to train more, starting from working on his fitness levels. A lot had to be done. After all, he was soon going to get the chance to play for his country for the very first time. And he was ready to give his all.

The feeling of debuting on the national stage was monumental. When he stepped onto the field wearing the colours of his country, he felt unstoppable. A climactic end to the match was served by the winning goal he scored against Pakistan, taking his team and country to a win. In that packed stadium, earning a name for India became one of the most memorable moments of his life. All those countless hours of practice were meant to get him to this day, it was all worth it. It was a feeling he never wanted to forget.

Slowly, a very important lesson was dawning on Sunil. Without hard work and a hunger to always improve, every talent was wasted. It was a lesson that would take him far in life.

The following year, as part of the national team, Sunil was training under a new coach. Bob Houghton was brought in to train the team after training competitive teams like China and Uzbekistan previously. He was also one of the youngest coaches to manage the English senior football. He brought with him many new ideas into the national team, such as managing proper nutrition, diet, fitness and rest. He also introduced the concept of training professionally into the Indian national team. And Sunil, ever eager for more, imbibed everything he could from Bob.

The mistakes and flaws that had ailed Sunil's game began to slowly disappear. Together they slowly began to build a national football team that was worth international recognition. One could even say Indian football was finally reborn!

4

SARDAR VALLABHBHAI PATEL

Forging a Nation Out of Chaos

Pandit Jawaharlal Nehru was not happy. He stared in dismay at the big piece of paper that lay before him. He and those who had fought with him for freedom had envisioned an undivided land that would break free from the yoke of British rule on the 15th of August 1947. That was how the final transfer of power, from the British was imagined to take place. Instead, what he saw was a far cry from the vision of the land that was to be free India. The map that was lying before him was not a consolidated land mass. Rather, a scattering of different states.

India before independence was divided into two types of territories for the ease of governance. In the first category were the territories that were directly ruled by the British. The second category comprised of the princely states, states that were internally ruled by hereditary rulers but were ultimately subject to the British Crown. A unification of both was to make up independent India.

However, there was a huge problem. The princely states, about 565 at the time, had no intention of coming under new governance when they had finally managed to break free of one. It was an open secret that the princely states would seize the moment of independence to declare self-rule. And they were right to do so since the Indian Independence Act 1947 stated that the rulers of the princely states had the option to accede to either of the newly born countries of India or Pakistan. They also had the option of continuing as a sovereign state. These states together formed close to fifty percent of pre-Independent India.

Without the princely states, the map of newly independent India looked bullet ridden, incomplete and absolutely unimaginable. Nehru clenched his fists. They had some time. The new Indian government would have to ensure that these 565 princely states acceded to India before the declaration of independence.

But who would undertake such a mammoth task? And why on earth would the rulers of the princely states agree to give up their power and submit to the rules of a democratically elected government? To make matters worse, India was dealing with problems on several fronts, partition being the greatest. The sheer violence it had unleashed was horrifying. It led to more communal riots and resettlement of refugees, all of which had already tested the fragile, still emerging set-up of law and order of the nation. If at such a time, the princely states chose to go their separate ways, India would never be able to get back up again.

The more Nehru thought of it, the sicker he felt. The task at hand required nerves of steel, an iron hand and yet a gentle spirit. Only one name came to his mind—Sardar Vallabhbhai Patel.

Vallabhbhai was not just the man who would go on to become the first Deputy Prime Minister and Home Minister of Independent India; he was a true follower of Gandhi and believed in his principles absolutely. A man with the reputation of being a go-getter, of simple habits and being an attentive listener, he was known to be the kind who got the job done. It was his display of leadership and empathy that earned him the prefix 'Sardar', a show of great love that the people of India had for him. Convinced there could be no better person to lead this tricky business, Sardar Vallabhbhai was sent the orders to set out on the mission. A mission he wasted no time to embark upon.

To convince the rulers of the princely states to join India rather than rule themselves was a hard line of thought to sell. Besides after about two centuries, the Indian princely rulers had become accustomed to the British style of rule. They were over-indulged and pampered by the British all the while getting exploited in the bargain. The Indian rulers had developed the thinking that they would be better off if they could govern their own affairs. To convince them to give up the right to rule their people, which they often considered divine, was not going to be without trouble.

Vallabhbhai had less than a year to accomplish his task before India officially became independent. And he held faith in V. P. Menon to be the man by his side.

V. P. Menon was an Indian Civil Servant who, among his other accomplishments, had been the Constitutional Adviser to three successive Viceroys before India finally became independent. As the political adviser to Lord Mountbatten at the time of independence, V. P. Menon's tact in solving the problems that had cropped up had greatly impressed Vallabhbhai. At the time the Indian National Congress and Muslim League had a total communication breakdown because the Muslim League proposed to partition the country into India and Pakistan. V. P. Menon was the man the Muslim League had approached to propose the plan to the Indian leaders.

His steady and calm attitude, diplomatic skills and ability to think on his feet were qualities that would prove to be a great asset when the princes were to be convinced to join India.

V. P. Menon immediately agreed to get on board as soon as he found out Vallabhbhai was at the helm of strategizing the mission. This was followed with Vallabhbhai seeking the blessings of Gandhi, as he always did at the start of something important.

"India, that is, Bharat, shall be a union of states." This union that Article 1 of the Indian constitution refers to was a direct result of the efforts of Sardar Patel. India, as the land it is today, owes a great deal to his vision and efforts. Surprisingly for Patel, who at one point in time did not even want to enter the field of politics.

Officially, Sardar Vallabhbhai Patel's birthday is believed to be on the 31st of October 1875. His real birthday he himself did not know. October 31st was a date he randomly gave when asked for one during his Matriculation exam. He was born into a farmer's family and spent his childhood in the small village of Karamsad in the Kheda district of Gujarat.

It was here that the young Vallabhbhai pursued his schooling and proved to be a good and diligent student. Barely had he seen anything of the world but he was sure he wanted to become a barrister and go study in England. But his family did not have enough money to help him realize this dream. While he pursued his studies, he was married to the young Jhaverba when he was just sixteen years old. Since it was his wish to be a barrister, he left his village to pursue higher studies in law at the age of twenty-two.

India at that time was a land ravaged by many diseases and extreme poverty. When a dear friend of Vallabhbhai got the plague, a highly infectious and dreaded disease that often led to death, he nursed his friend to good health. As a result of which he too fell ill. Instead of heading home to get well, he went and stayed in an old derelict temple so that he would not infect anyone else. He recuperated and got better on his own. Only then did he go back home to his worried family.

Soon he began practicing law, and soon another tragedy followed his life. Vallabhbhai was in court cross-examining a witness, when a messenger brought him a note bearing terrible news. His beloved wife had passed away. Despite her successful surgery for cancer, she had died in the hospital. Vallabhbhai read the note, placed it in his pocket, took a moment to collect himself and resumed his cross-examination. He did not let anyone know about his great loss at that moment. But a testament to his love for Jhaverba was how he never forgot her and never re-married all his life.

A year later, in 1910 Vallabhbhai left for England to study for Barristership. He had to overcome many challenges to be able to do so. The course was of three years at Middle Temple. He immersed himself in his studies and keenly observed the way of life of the British; it was a fascinating experience for him. Working hard as ever he managed to complete the 36-month course in 30 months and also topped his class.

By 1913, it was time to head home. But Vallabhbhai's stint in England had changed him in one way. So impressed had he become by the ways of the English that he came back completely anglicized. He now chose to talk only in English, he changed his clothes to English suits at all times, and he also developed the habit of smoking cigars. On returning, Vallabhbhai settled down in Ahmedabad and began his practice as a Barrister. Diligence and steadiness established him as a leading criminal lawyer, soon money and fame followed.

Life was finally going smooth now. He often heard of Gandhiji's fight for independence but did not believe in his methods. He was immersed in his work and often went to the Gujarat Club in Ahmedabad in the evenings to play Bridge, a card game. On one such evening, Gandhiji happened to visit the club for a speech. But Vallabhbhai did not go to listen to him, choosing instead to concentrate on his game. When his dear friend G. V. Mavlankar, an independence activist, who was also playing with him, wanted to go and listen to Gandhiji, Vallabhbhai countered him, asking, "What difference would it make?"

"Gandhiji would ask you if you know how to sift pebbles from wheat and that is supposed to bring independence," mocked Vallabhbhai, unaware that everything he believed in was about to change.

In the year 1917, the farmers in the Champaran district of Bihar were revolting against the British. They were being forced to grow Indigo, a crop that used copious amounts of water to grow, was bought by the British at dirt cheap prices only to be sold for huge profits. It often left the soil severely depleted and almost infertile. At this point, Gandhiji channeled the anger of the farmers by organizing mass protests peacefully. Also called the Champaran or Kheda Satyagraha, it gained immediate popularity among Indians.

Vallabhbhai too read about it and was tremendously inspired. But it was a meeting with Gandhiji soon after, that convinced him that he needed to join the Indian movement for independence. When Gandhiji needed someone to lead the Kheda Satyagraha after him, he chose Vallabhbhai. Coming from a family of peasants, Vallabhbhai could assess the situation of the farmers with more empathy. It changed the direction of his life. Working with his countrymen and ensuring they were given justice became a cause he wanted to stand for with all his force—he had found a purpose to lead him on.

If there were any doubts in his mind, they were removed with the news of the Jallianwala Bagh incident in Amritsar. A crowd of unarmed, peaceful protesters had gathered to protest against the arrest of their heroes who were fighting for Indian independence. Thousands of people had gathered in the garden that had only one exit. Instead of warning them to disperse, the Brigadier General in-charge at that time, R. E. H. Dyer, ordered his army to open fire. Bullets rained down on men, women and children who had no way left to save themselves. No one was warned; no one was spared. The death toll was estimated to be more than 1,200. The monstrous act shook everyone. General Dyer was let off without being held accountable for his actions. And the people had had enough.

Vallabhbhai was now deeply committed to the cause of overthrowing British rule forever. When Gandhiji began his non-violent, Non-cooperation movement, Vallabhbhai was at the forefront. Overnight, he gave up his English ways. He organized bonfires all over Ahmedabad and exhorted people to publicly burn British possessions. He himself burnt all his

English clothes, articles and books, choosing to wear clothes handspun in the Indian Khadi.

There was no looking back from this point. He became an active member of the Indian National Congress, in which role he managed events of tremendous scale undaunted. When he was elected as the President of the Ahmedabad Municipal Board, the surprised city woke up one morning to the news that their President was not just figuratively, but literally out on a cleaning mission. Vallabhbhai, broom in hand, was busy cleaning the most neglected areas of the city–the parts where the 'untouchables' lived.

This simple act won over the hearts of the people. Vallabhbhai immediately began to work on improving the archaic sanitation and drainage facilities in the city. He also improved the water storage and distribution infrastructure. The city began to look up to him as its savior. But it was the peasant protests of 1927 organized by Vallabhbhai in Bardoli that captured the imagination of the entire nation.

The peasants of Bardoli were burdened with unrealistic taxes by the British and when they pleaded for mercy, not only were they refused but the percentage of taxes was raised further. When Vallabhbhai was asked to lead the protests, he organized an impactful non-violent movement that had the British eventually back out. Not only was the revenue payment for that year cancelled but the increase in taxes was put off until the year after the next. In addition, the lands that the British had confiscated from the protesting farmers were returned to them. This was a major victory for Vallabhbhai and his method of leadership. And the nation took note. So great was the esteem Indians held him in that now people began to attach the term '*Sardar*' before his name. In Vallabhbhai they had found a *leader* they looked up to and admired.

Vallabhbhai continued to serve the people of the nation and the Indian National Congress. He became particularly devoted to Gandhiji and was even jailed along with him in the year 1932. Not one to while away time, he learnt Sanskrit from Gandhiji while in prison. For Vallabhbhai, the word of Gandhiji was now the word of law. He had come a long way from when he believed Gandhiji's way of independence was to sift pebbles from wheat!

Finally, the time India had waited for centuries was arriving. *At the stroke of the midnight hour*, India would rise to its freedom on the 15th of August 1947. Pandit Jawaharlal Nehru was set to become the first Prime Minister, Vallabhbhai was to be the first Deputy Prime Minister and Home Minister of free India. He was to handle the States Department and the Information and Broadcasting Ministry. In this capacity, Vallabhbhai had to shoulder the huge responsibility of the accession of princely states to India.

If the princely states did not agree to join the union, independence would turn out to be a hollow victory. This task would prove to be the greatest test for Sardar Patel. A band of leaders were watching him, anticipating a success that could unify a country now free. So how did he make it happen?

With V. P. Menon, Vallabhbhai first drafted a legal document that came to be known as 'The Instrument of Accession'. This would enable the princely states to officially become part of India. They would effectively be giving control of the defense, communication and foreign affairs of their states to the central government. In return, the country would fix an annual allowance to be given to them. This was called a Privy Purse.

Vallabhbhai now explained to V. P. Menon the method they would use to talk, coax, cajole and convince the princes. While he would take care of strategizing how each princely state needs to be approached, Menon would work on the ground, ensuring the smooth implementation of the said strategy. Five hundred sixty-five princes had to be convinced and the land of a free country was at stake.

Over the course of the next few months, Vallabhbhai arranged several luncheons in honour of the rulers of these princely states. To make the rulers feel like stakeholders in the formation of a new nation, they were all invited to help the Indian National Congress frame the Constitution of independent India. They were made to feel a part of the momentous occasion that was about to occur. Vallabhbhai reminded them of the debt they owed their motherland in a bid to get them to sign the Instrument of Accession. Also, they were made aware of how chaotic their kingdoms could get in the absence of proper rule. How would they manage on their own should their populations incite revolts? Vallabhbhai told them that under Central rule, their kingdoms would make far more progress than they could hope to on their own.

The Privy Purse was an offer made to the princes in exchange for them signing the Instrument. The rulers were reluctant initially, but Vallabhbhai was very persuasive. He was ready to clear any of their doubts, allay any fears they had and assure them that this was the right thing to do.

As a result, an overwhelming majority of princes agreed to the terms placed before them and signed. This essentially meant that now their independent states would cease to be. All the villages, land and palaces of the rulers was to become the property of the Indian Government. Besides, they handed over collectively a railway system of 12,000 miles to the nation. And they did this before they had even received any compensation for it!

The 15th of August 1947 was a moment of true pride for India when a united nation with most of the princely states, got independence. Vallabhbhai and V. P. Menon had achieved a remarkable feat. However, some states had not formally signed the Instrument thereby not becoming a part of India… yet.

Each of these princely states had to be dealt with in a different manner. And sure enough, Vallabhbhai adopted different tactics to convince them that joining India was the right thing to do.

Under pressure from Vallabhbhai, a small state in central India—hence vital to the land, Piploda finally signed the Instrument of Accession in March 1948. Maharaja Hanvant Singh had newly ascended the throne in Jodhpur just before independence. His predecessor had committed to join India. But with the advice of his councilors, the Maharaja began to have second thoughts. Since he was inexperienced and relatively young, he was lured by better prospects offered by Pakistan with whom Jodhpur shared a common border. When Vallabhbhai got wind of the situation, he met Hanvant Singh urgently with several benefits for the Maharaja from the Indian government.

While Vallabhbhai wooed Hanvant Singh, he was also not afraid to speak frankly. He warned Singh that should he still decide to join Pakistan, he would be violating the whole idea of a two-nation theory that had been introduced by Jinnah. The theory emphasized a separate nation for

Muslims in the subcontinent. It was the reason Pakistan came into existence. He told Hanvant clearly that communal violence could become a real problem for him if he chose to go ahead with Pakistan since Jodhpur had a predominantly Hindu population. Ultimately, Maharaja Hanvant Singh, considering all circumstances, chose to accede to India.

The case of the princely state of Junagadh was different. Nawab Muhammad Mahabat Khanji III ruled a population that was 20% Muslim and 80% Hindu. Despite constant attempts by V. P. Menon and Vallabhbhai, the Nawab had decided to accede to Pakistan on 15th of September 1947. When the Hindu population of Junagadh got wind of the fact that they were not going to be a part of independent India, they caused a huge unrest.

So great was their anger directed at the Nawab that he had to leave his own kingdom and run for his life. The Nawab and his family escaped to Karachi in Pakistan where they were given asylum. Pakistan then encouraged the Nawab to form a provisional government of Junagadh in Pakistan. Since the Nawab was the head of state, it was natural that the seat of his government would be where he is, which essentially meant Junagadh had acceded to Pakistan.

Vallabhbhai now requested Pakistan to treat the Accession of Junagadh as invalid. He proposed that a plebiscite—public vote to decide on an important matter—be held in Junagadh to determine what the people of the state wanted. Pakistan rejected the offer and was now forced to deal with the tough side of Vallabhbhai. He sent the Indian Army into Junagadh on 1st November 1947 to take control of the state. A plebiscite was then held in December. The result was a 99% vote of the public in favour of accession to India.

There was another princely state where a Hindu king, Maharaja Hari Singh, ruled a Muslim majority. The Maharaja was reluctant to join Kashmir with India or Pakistan. India on its part considered Kashmir a very important state since it shared international borders with a number of countries like Tibet, China and Afghanistan. Like India, Pakistan too had its sights set on Kashmir and wanted it desperately. While the Maharaja delayed his decision, the situation in Kashmir became unruly with Pakistan's interference.

Vallabhbhai, in an attempt to send a message to Pakistan, took a number of steps to send a clear signal to Pakistan. Srinagar was included in the air route of a number of flights. Srinagar was connected to the rest of the nation by telephone and telegraph lines laid in the Pathankot, Amritsar and Jammu triangle. The Indian Army was posted in several strategic regions around Kashmir should it be needed.

Pakistan soon realized that it needed to do more to bring Kashmir into its fold. On 22nd October 1947 more than 5000 Pakistani soldiers known as Lashkars infiltrated Kashmir and marched towards Srinagar. Maharaja Hari Singh fought them back bravely with his own army but two days later he was at a clear disadvantage. He then desperately sent a message to Vallabhbhai asking for help in fending off the Pakistanis. In return, he was ready to sign the Instrument of Accession.

Vallabhbhai immediately had V. P. Menon fly down to Jammu so that the Maharaja could sign the Instrument. Meanwhile he arranged an emergency meeting of the Indian Defense Committee with the Defense Minister Shri Baldev Singh and Prime Minister Nehru in attendance. They decided that the Indian troops that had been posted in the valley were to mount a defense against the Pakistanis.

But things were not going to be easy. The Army could not move with all its equipment and arms since the only motorable road link to Jammu ran through Sialkot in Pakistan. That link had been cut off. Once again Vallabhbhai thought on his feet. He decided that the road would have to be rebuilt. In what seemed like an impossible task, Vallabhbhai collected the material in a matter of fifteen days. Workers to make the road were brought in by special trains. They worked round the clock to get the road functioning.

By December of that year, Pakistan had been given a huge setback by the Indian Army. They were pushed back beyond the river Jhelum. Kashmir was safe and now a part of independent India.

The largest state territorially in British India was Hyderabad. It was also the richest. The Nizam Osman Ali however refused to join India. Despite innumerable attempts by Vallabhbhai and mediators, the Nizam refused to accede. On the other hand, he quietly kept importing arms and ammunition from Europe and increasing his army.

Vallabhbhai did not retaliate until the day the Razakars initiated violence against the Hindu population of the princely state. The Razakars, an undisciplined and violent volunteer force, were committed to the cause of maintaining Muslim rule in Hyderabad and resisting all attempts to accede to India.

Under 'Operation Polo', armed forces were sent to Hyderabad on 17th September 1948. They entered Hyderabad from five directions, engaged with the Razakars for four days, at the end of which the Razakars surrendered.

The Nizam agreed to disband his Razakar army and accede to India soon after.

A beautiful territory made up of 36 islands and several coral reefs, lush in natural beauty and aquatic life, Lakshwadeep was eyed by both Pakistan and India for accession specifically due to its strategic location. Cut off from the mainland, the inhabitants on the island were barely even aware of independence. Pakistan tried to make its move by sending its Navy to capture the island. However, as soon as Vallabhbhai got information about it, he sent the Indian Navy to defend the island. The Pakistanis were fought off and Lakshwadeep acceded to India.

Places like Pondicherry, Karaikal, Yanam, Mahe, Chandernagore were still colonies of France. Goa, Daman and Diu, Dadra and Nagar Haveli were colonies of Portugal. All these too would eventually become a part of India in a few years.

With the princely states now a solid part of India, Vallabhbhai had done what no other man had accomplished. He had formed a nation out of separate states. It was a task on a magnitude not seen before or since. The nation was proud of her son and yet Vallabhbhai did not slow the pace of his work nor his devotion to Gandhiji. Once, when he was asked by Gandhiji about what he wanted to do post-independence, he said he would like to become a monk.

However, fate had other plans. Two months after Gandhiji was shot, Vallabhbhai too passed away.

Vallabhbhai forged a nation out of scattered states. Sixty-eight years later, the country honoured him with the tallest statue in the world, The Statue of Unity. A statue so high, mirroring the immense respect, love and admiration the country and its people will have for him forever.

5

JADAV PAYENG

The Lone Ranger

"Run over? By hundreds of elephants?" asked Gunin Saikia incredulously. As the Assistant Conservator of Forests in the Jorhat province of the state of Assam, he was in-charge of the well-being of several forests in the state. Silently, he looked at the villager from head to toe, assessing if he was high on Apo, the locally brewed liquor famous among the village tribes.

Clad in a simple *kurta* and mud-stained *dhoti*, it would have taken the villager more than five hours to reach the Forest office so he could lodge his complaint. He couldn't be drunk or lying, Gunin thought. But the story he told seemed so hard to believe that he had no choice but to look at him through eyes of doubt. The villager was claiming hundreds of elephants had passed through the crops of the people of Arun Chapori in order to get to the jungle. Since the village lay on the edge of the jungle, the elephants had damaged their homes as well.

Gunin took his job seriously and what's more—he loved it. Over the decades that spanned his career, he had made a considerable difference in the population and quality of trees that grew in the state. His work involved managing forests, preventing forest fires, protecting the green cover of the state and even helping the villagers co-exist with wild animals. That was why the villager from Arun Chapori was standing before him right now. And while Gunin was sympathetic to the woes of this man, he could not ignore the anomalies in his story.

Majuli, the supposed location of the jungle, was a barren river island where nothing could grow. Gunin would know. Many years ago, the Social Forest Division had tried to introduce a plan to plant trees on the Majuli sandbar and had failed since the land was barren. If the trees could not grow and survive there, how could there be a jungle? And since there was no jungle, how could there be elephants? In fact, there hadn't been elephants in that part of the state for decades now. The details did not add up. Something was clearly amiss.

What is more, Gunin was having a particularly busy day. Just back from a survey of trees that had to be marked for felling, he now had to decide when the annual tree counting was to begin, his orders were awaited for commencing the annual spraying of pesticides on the trees and he also had to undertake the examination of nurseries, timber depots, and plantations. He was occupied by these tasks when the villager from Arun Chapori had turned up and made such inconceivable allegations.

The course of action was clear. He would have to drop everything and go to Majuli Island to find out for himself just what was going on.

Gunin set out with his team to Arun Chapori. It was going to be a long, long day…

Majuli is an island in the middle of the river Brahmaputra. It is the largest such river-island in the world. And while it was the river that gave birth to the island, it is the very river that is the reason for the island remaining barren. Every year, the Brahmaputra swells to gigantic proportions during the monsoon, bringing plenty of water with incredible force and carrying away the fertile topsoil of vast areas of the land. As a result, every year, hundreds of acres of land is rendered barren, unable to support any form of life.

To save the topsoil of the island, the Social Forestry Wing of the Assam State Forest Department had begun an experiment in the year 1980. They began a program to measure how well trees could protect the island from floods and erosion. A period of five years was marked to plant as many trees as possible in roughly about five hundred acres of land on Arun Chapori which was a barren sandbar situated in the middle of the Brahmaputra. But three years later, the progress was slow and the money to fund the project had run out. The unpaid labourers abandoned the project and Arun Chapori remained vulnerable to floods and erosion.

As soon as the ferry reached the island of Majuli, the villager who had been quiet all this while suddenly came to life, confident that his problems would be redressed. He led the way from the ferry towards his village, all the while telling Gunin stories of how the elephants had begun to frequent the area a few years ago, how the tigers had begun to kill the cows in the village and the cows they took to graze in the jungle. He even told them that the villagers were so angry that they were planning to make the person responsible for the jungle, pay a very heavy price.

The Forest Department team was now more curious than ever. But for all the stories of the villager, they saw nothing but barren land so far. Gunin was beginning to worry that they may have wasted their time on nothing. And then the village of Arun Chapori came into view.

Arun Chapori was like a hamlet consisting of about one hundred and ninety four people in all. The main source of occupation here was either farming or rearing cows and cattle. On meeting the villagers, Gunin and his team asked them about the damage to their crops and homes due to the animals. And they had a lot to say. One villager began to weep telling Gunin how a tiger had carried away his only source of income, his cow. Another began to show the damaged hut he was living out of since the elephants had started coming. Soon all the villagers were cursing a man named Mola for being the reason for this mess.

They asked to see the damaged crops from where they could trace footprints of the elephants and figure out where they had gone. Sure enough, there were imprints of large animal feet across a few farms, stunning the Forest Department team now. They eagerly began to follow the footprints which soon brought into their view the largest imaginable group of trees they had ever expected to find on this land they had thought was infertile.

As they went closer, Gunin realized that this was no cluster of a few trees or even a couple of acres of forest. This was thick foliage, a dense wall of creepers, bushes, trees and grass. He had to stop for a moment and steady himself. This could not be possible. And yet here he was, about to enter a jungle that wasn't even supposed to be here. Gunin could feel the strain of the journey evaporate as he walked into *Mola'r Haabi*. Mola's Forest.

As they approached the forest they were touched by the feeling of awe and delight. Gunin began to chuckle, prompting his team to look at him suspiciously. “Just how big is this place?” he asked the villager. “Sahab, I don’t know the precise area but it is more than thousands of acres,” replied the villager not sure of the reaction of the officers he had brought with him. They were supposed to help with the loss of his people. Instead, they were amazed by the very source of their problems. What’s more, Gunin was grinning now on hearing this.

A few rabbits scurried by as Gunin and his team entered Mola’r Haabi and a flock of parrots flew away frightened by the sudden disturbance. Even the air here seemed different. “It feels like… there is more air in the air here,” said Gunin and his team agreed, wholeheartedly endorsing that he was not imagining it. He spotted trees of Bamboo, Neem, Guava, Banyan, Custard Apple, Indian Rosewood even. Gunin’s head was reeling from the discovery. Valcol, Arjun, Mulberry, Pride of India were just some of the varieties Gunin and his team passed by. A gentle breeze rustled the leaves as if welcoming them.

Just then his reverie was broken by loud noises. They heard voices coming from a distance and the sound of metal striking wood. This could only mean one thing—thieves or poachers at work. The team’s training kicked into action. Without another word, they began to sprint in the direction of the growing voices…

The sickening sound of the metal hitting wood was echoing everywhere. And Jadav heard it too.

He was well through half his day as he tried to coax a few saplings he had recently planted, to grow healthier. He added some more cow dung which he used as manure for the plants.

Then, he double checked the earthen pots he had placed near these new saplings for water supply. Since Jadav did not have access to running water to irrigate the trees and shrubs, he had made and perfected his own system of ensuring the seeds and saplings were well watered even if he could not water them every single day.

He looked at the Mango grove nearby and they were inviting him to come and rest for a while in their shade. Jadav had felt the trees use their leaves to speak to each other, to him and to the wind too. Like when trees would sense the approach of moisture bearing clouds and their leaves would stop the clouds and make it rain on them. Jadav lived in amazement of this marvelous ingenuity of Mother Nature.

Suddenly he was shaken out of his thoughts by a sickening thud. He knew what it meant. On hearing the sound of trees being cut, he froze suddenly as he tried to assess where the sound was coming from. And he began to run too.

As he got closer, he could hear agitated voices and more trees being hit by axes. He too had wondered if there were thieves. But to his dismay, when he got there, he saw a small mob of villagers, intent on chopping down trees that Jadav had painstakingly spent his life growing. The anger of the villagers would have made any sane man want to stay away. But Jadav had to save the forest, no matter the cost.

Without a thought to his life, the slightly built Jadav rushed to the mob shouting for them to stop and placed himself squarely between the villagers and the trees. He was within striking distance and one swoop of the axe was all it would have taken to bring him down. From the other side, the villager along with Gunin and his subordinates came running to the site of the commotion.

Taken by surprise, the villagers paused. But they were not going to back off. Not this time. The tension in the air was thick; one couldn't sever it with a knife.

Ignoring the latest entrants to the site, the eldest spoke up, "Step out of our way Molai, today we are not going to listen to you." Jadav winced at the use of the name he was given as a child. It meant 'winter radish' since as a child his cheeks would often turn pink, just like the vegetable. These were people who had seen him grow up. They had been witness to the task he had set out on. Opposing them would be hard, but this madness had to stop. He could not let them destroy the forest. He replied, "Very well, if you wish I will not say a word. But you cannot cut a single tree from here. Not for as long as I am alive," he finished, an assertive finality marking his words.

"Can't cut a single tree as long as you are alive? Why, because you planted this forest? You did it for your own satisfaction Molai. But what about us, why are we paying the price for this hobby of yours? Just last night, a tiger attacked yet another one of my cows," said a farmer whose loss was so fresh that tears sprung to his eyes. Another one broke in, "Do you know that this is the ninth cow that we have lost in this year? Not just us, but all the other villages near this forest are suffering too." And yet a third complained, "If it is not the tigers, then we have to worry about the elephants. We have all lost so much of our crops due to the elephants that come here. Even our homes are not spared sometimes. How long will we suffer silently? Molai, the way we see it, this jungle has to go," he concluded. And then, with renewed determination, he lifted his axe.

Jadav was a patient man and heard them all silently. He knew they were not wrong, but their solution wasn't right either. There was only one thing to do. He stood his ground. There was a steely determination in his eyes that made it difficult for all those present to ignore him.

His words echoed in the breeze that began to blow almost as if the trees were upset too. Jadav said, "Each tree here is my child. Which parent will stand by mutely when his children are being killed and that too by his own people?"

The simplicity with which Jadav had confronted the villagers was heartening for Gunin to see. Here was one man standing his ground against a small, angry mob, all so he could save the trees. Then, the farmer whose cow had just been attacked this morning threw down his axe. Dejection was all over his face as his legs gave away and he sat down.

Jadav now looked at all of them and said, "Cutting the trees is not the answer to this problem. Instead of creating a path that keeps the elephants away from our villages, you want to take away their food? Instead of fencing in and protecting our cows and cattle better, you want to take away their home and kill them? You say the jungle is bad, but you forget that the reason you can grow your crops and rear your cattle is the jungle. Was this not barren land that only became fertile once the trees began to take root here? Is it not true that every year, the Brahmaputra River would be flooded and as a result, wash away hundreds of kilometers of fertile soil if it were not for the roots of the trees of this jungle that you now want to uproot?"

Among the group of villagers were small children too, who had tagged along just to see what was going on. Jadav looked at the young boys, about four of them and asked, "Is this the world we want to leave behind for them? Where cutting trees is the easier way out instead of growing them?"

Jadav then went up to the farmer who had lost his cow and said, "It would be so much better to protect our cows instead of cutting the trees or killing the tigers. Take wood from here and create a secure fence for your cattle. And as far as the elephants are concerned, they will not bother you now. I have grown enough bamboo for them here that they will not need to wander to your crops to feed themselves."

Gunin was very impressed. In the simplest manner, Jadav had proved yet again to these men that nature was not the root cause of their problems. In fact, it held the solution to their many problems. The villagers began to leave but one young boy of about eight or nine years, stayed back. He stared curiously at Jadav until he was called out by his father.

One of Gunin's subordinates spoke up now. "Who are you and have you grown all of this yourself?" Jadav smiled on hearing that and said, "My name is Jadav Payeng and no, I have not grown all these trees, they have grown by themselves." No sooner had Jadav said this, everyone burst into smiles. Gunin introduced himself saying, "I am Gunin Saikia, Assistant Conservator of Forests from Jorhat. And Jadav, what you have done here is nothing short of a miracle. It is truly our pleasure to meet you. Can we talk?"

Jadav led them through the thicket into a small clearing where there was a hut, a damaged one, however. Jadav told them that this was where he lived and even his hut had been destroyed a bit by the elephants. Gunin asked Jadav how he was so calm when his home too had been broken by the very creatures he was trying to protect.

"I have a question for you too. Nature has made a food chain. Why can't we follow it? Once, a leopard dragged away three buffaloes of mine that were grazing in the forest. But I didn't try to stop it. Because that is the way nature has intended leopards to be. When a herd of elephants passes by, it is best to hide because only a fool would stand before wild elephants. You see, this is all God's way of ensuring nature runs its course. If you and I begin to hunt these animals down, who will protect them?"

It was an argument Gunin found hard to challenge. As a protector of forests himself, he was glad to find a kindred spirit who had achieved such a massive feat all on his own. "What led you to do this Jadav Payeng? Tell us everything."

Jadav ensured his guests were comfortable on a cot that lay outside his home. He then said, "Okay, but let me get you all some tea first. I have learnt that stories sound far more interesting with some chai in hand." His guests broke into smiles, their piles of work at Jorhat forgotten, for what they had found here was so much more valuable.

The waning sunlight gave way to the evening making the jungle look different now. It would definitely get colder as the night fell, thought Gunin. They could hear the calls of different birds while monkeys chattered in the trees. At a distance peacocks called out to each other. There was immense comfort just by sitting here. Jadav had created heaven on the barren earth. While they waited for him, Gunin identified more varieties of trees like Flame of the Forest, Moj, Silk, Teak and even Cotton.

Once Jadav returned, he handed them all small steel tea glasses and said, "Sahab, do you know that this particular area where we are, is of great historical importance? It is called Mohgorh Khuti. The first Burma War between the Burmese and the British was fought here in the year 1826. Later, the British laid the first railway track here and called it the Jorhat Provincial Railway. They also made a dockyard here. As a child, I remember seeing ships bring goods here from Kolkata and Dhaka too. But between 1965 and 1970, all of this was washed away by the Brahmaputra. The erosion was of such extent that ten kilometres of good soil was carried away in the waters of the great river and Mohgorh Khuti became barren. I just wanted to bring back the place of my childhood, the place that was lush and green, like it is now."

They talked for long and when it was time to go back, Gunin had decided that this place deserved to be protected. He made a mental note to put in an application for special status to be granted to Mola'r Haabi. The forest was a miracle but the man who grew it was destined for much more. Of that, Gunin was certain.

Alone now, Jadav began to inspect the damage that had been inflicted to his hut. It would take him a couple of days to mend it. So Jadav decided to stay in the jungle for the night.

For many, the jungle could be a scary place, but for Jadav, the trees and all the creatures here were his children. To him, this was home. He lit a small bonfire and settled on his charpoy. As he stared at the star laden sky through the thick foliage of the trees, his mind went to all that had occurred today and then, to all that had brought him here…

He was born in 1963 in the small village of Kokilamukh near Jorhat town on Majuli Island. The state of Assam consists of many native tribes; Jadav was a native of the Mishing tribe.

The Mishing were a group of people who thought of the forest as their home. Their main source of income was to rear cattle and sell milk—what Jadav was meant to do too for the rest of his life. He grew up loving Mother Earth and all her creations—the rivers, the mountains, the trees and the animals. Jadav would spend hours in the forests, picking fruits from trees or chasing monkeys and birds. Or he would go swimming in the cool and inviting waters of the Brahmaputra. But while growing up, he saw the forests beginning to disappear. With the forests gone, even the animals and birds were gone. He was witnessing the happy place of his childhood turn into a dull, grey and colourless place.

Like everyone else, he could have accepted the gradual decline of the greenery everywhere as a price for development. But the loss of the forest sparked in him a keen interest in plants, which really took wings when a young Jadav met Jadabesh Barua, an agricultural scientist.

Jadav's school was in the nearby village of Nobinang Boligaon. There he met Dr Barua who loved teaching young children about plants through real life lessons. He would give the young children saplings and ask them to plant them. The doctor saw that Jadav had a special knack for taking care of these plants, especially the Betel or *Paan* plant which is very difficult to grow.

It became a regular for the Doctor to hand over a number of saplings under Jadav's care. He would also give Jadav twenty-five paisa as a reward. Being a child, Jadav would often spend this money on groundnuts and chomp on the fruits of his labour for hours. One day, when Dr Barua asked Jadav what he did with the money, he was amused by Jadav's answer. He then took Jadav's hand and told him that by spending the money on groundnuts, Jadav was only taking care of himself. If, however, he spent that money on buying and planting trees, he would be able to take care of himself, his family, his village, his country and the planet. His words went on to change Jadav's worldview in profound ways, making him understand the connection between people and nature. Caring for nature was to care for oneself and other people. From then on, it became common for Jadav to plant a seed here, a sapling there.

In 1979 however, an incident in his life strengthened this understanding, changing the course of his life forever. The floods of Brahmaputra that year brought hundreds of water snakes from China and Arunachal Pradesh, onto the Majuli sandbar. The sixteen-year-old was fascinated by them. However, the next day, the water receded and all the snakes were left dead. Jadav was stunned. He cried like he had never cried before, sitting there on the dry sandbar, next to the dead snakes, reflecting on the carnage. *Was this the fate that awaited us all?*

Now, Jadav was even more determined to make a change. He came upon the idea to alert the forest department to do something about the matter. In response, he was told that since the land on Majuli was barren, they would be unable to do much. He also began to consult his elders who belonged to different tribes. Some of the elders from the Deori tribe advised him to grow Bamboo trees. Bamboo is the world's tallest grass and can house snakes with ease. Not just that, the elders handed him fifty bamboo seeds and some saplings. They told him to plant these and save the snakes. Jadav was overjoyed. Here was something he could do on his own, when everyone else thought there was no scope to fix things for the island.

But there was one small problem. Getting to the sandbar involved a half an hour walk to the river followed by a boat ride. On getting to Majuli, Jadav would walk another two hours before he reached the sandbar. But resolute in his plan, nothing could discourage him. He first decided to give up school. Next, he built himself a boat with the help of his elders. He was unaware then, how this boat would come to carry him to Majuli all his life.

Every day, the sixteen-year-old Jadav began to make the four-hour trek to Majuli Island with his precious Bamboo. He enthusiastically planted his grass here, but he soon realised merely doing that would not be enough. In an environment that was hostile to life, he would have to ensure that the seeds and saplings were well watered. Once again he consulted his elders. They had lived in harmony with nature all their lives; he expected them to have the answers he was looking for. They gave him the idea to make holes in earthen pots, stuff them with hay, and then fill the pots with water. He would mount these earthen pots on bamboo platforms that would drip water onto the seed or sapling in small and steady quantities. Jadav would go there every day to ensure that these pots were regularly refilled. He also ensured that the plants got enough manure and used cow dung for this purpose.

Jadav had found his aim in life. He began to work tirelessly towards re-foresting Majuli with bamboo. People thought he was crazy to even think of doing something on such a scale. He also constantly sought the assistance of the Forest Department. His pleas were finally answered in 1980 in the form of the project undertaken by the Social Forestry Wing of the Assam State Forest Department to re-forest about five-hundred acres of eroded land near Arun Chapori. They were looking for labourers and Jadav immediately signed up for the task. For three years, the planters worked tirelessly to grow trees on the piece of land but eventually the project ran short of funds. The result was that it was abandoned as all the labourers decided to leave; all but one.

Jadav refused to quit. He was determined to not just take care of the trees that had been planted but also plant new ones. The Brahmaputra was the source of so much erosion but Jadav never overlooked the fact that it was the river itself that brought along with it lots of seeds and plants from upstream and deposited them ashore. Jadav would sift through them and plant the ones he was confident would survive.

To keep his promise to Mother Earth, he left his home and began to live on the sandbar itself. It was an isolated existence. But it wasn't a lonely one, because he had his trees and plants for company. This work, however, was not short of challenges. Now, the sandbar was lush with Bamboo but the other trees often found it difficult to thrive. Although the seeds took root, the saplings were not growing healthy enough. From more manure to more water to pesticides, he had tried everything. It was not easy to keep the trees healthy.

One evening, a vexed Jadav was sitting with the elders in his village. They took a lot of interest in what he was up to and when he told them that apart from Bamboo, everything else he grew wasn't faring well, there was silence all around. "Have you tried Amroli?" one toothless elderly man casually questioned as he sipped on his Apo. Jadav's eyes widened, he had not thought about Amroli or red ants. The elderly man continued, "When ants dig tunnels, they aerate the soil allowing water to reach the roots of the plants better. It also helps in mixing nutrients in the soil so that…" but he never got to the end of his sentence. Jadav leapt up and hugged him so tight that all he could manage was a toothless grin.

The suggestion, however, proved easier said than done. From the next day, Jadav was all over the place, trying to catch red ants. He would collect them in a sack and carry them to Majuli Island. The children of the village had made a game of it, the minute they spotted an ant hill, they would begin calling out to Jadav who had by now lost count of the number of times he had been stung. Jadav also devised another, less painful way, to make the land fertile. He released earthworms into the soil of Majuli. The earthworms would burrow deep, loosening the hardened soil that made it easier for water to reach the roots. Also, by feeding on dead leaves, the earthworms would leave behind organic waste that provided nutrition to plants.

Raising the trees was all that mattered to Jadav. And in doing so, he lost track of time. Days turned to weeks which gave way to years. And slowly, the trees became a thriving jungle. It also began to attract wildlife. First a few birds, rabbits and even snakes. And then they came in huge numbers. Birds from the nearby areas as well as migratory ones began to make this jungle their home. Soon the Indian Rhinos, Bengal Tigers, monkeys of different species, deer, rabbits, peacocks and hundreds of elephants started inhabiting the forest which was now referred to by the locals as *Mola'r Haabi* or *Molai Khatoni*.

But to Jadav, it mattered little what the forest was called. For him, this was his home too. All he wanted was for it to grow bigger and greener. For all the animals that sought refuge in it, to stay safe and unharmed, even if that meant repairing his hut a hundred times.

In the year 2007, a young wildlife photographer and journalist named Jitu Kalita chanced upon the forest and made it quite famous. But no one, least of all Jadav, had expected *Mola'r Haabi* to become national and then international news, once the Forest Department team visited it. Soon, he was featured in innumerable articles, a movie and several documentaries. He began to receive invitations to travel to Indian and foreign cities, with everyone around him wanting to know the same thing that Gunin and his team had: how did he do it?

The attention unnerved the quiet and shy Jadav who was most comfortable in the wild. The papers said he had managed to create a man-made forest greater than Central Park. Little did he know that the story of his feat would soon be included in the schools of the very country Central Park was in!

While Jadav certainly did not want this attention, he realized that it came with a very heavy price. The jungle had become a target for wildlife poaching and on the hit list of the hunters was the Indian Rhino. This majestic one-horned animal is an endangered species, much sought after for its horn, the extraction of which kills the rhino. When the news of the presence of rhinos in *Mola'r Haabi* broke, naturally hunters from all over began to make forays into the jungle, posing another difficulty in Jadav's work.

It was then that Jadav asked for the help of the Forest Department to fight the poaching menace. The Forest Rangers patrolled the jungle and ensured that the animals could live in a secure habitat. Jadav made it a lifelong habit to stay ever vigilant. All the while, he kept planting and nurturing the forest.

Soon, he began to receive invitations from countries like France, Switzerland, Bangladesh, Taiwan and countries from the Middle East. They requested him to come and teach them how to grow their own forests. In the face of all the fame, Jadav never forgot his roots. He accepted the invitations and spread across the world his beliefs about Mother Earth. That taking care of it meant caring for ourselves, and the generations to come.

In the year 2012, Jawaharlal Nehru University, one of India's premier educational institutes, invited Jadav to their campus. There, his knowledge of wildlife was assessed by experts. Jadav was asked questions on every imaginable topic related to the forest and by the end of three days Jadav had left the experts speechless with his practical knowledge. They honoured him with the title of 'The Forest Man of India'. An award by the great A. P. J. Abdul Kalam, the then president of India, followed. And in 2015, Jadav Payeng was awarded the Padma Shri, the fourth highest civilian honour in India. While he was grateful for the recognition his work gave him, in the quietness of his home, the awards must have not seemed any charming. His focus was just how he could use all his time and money on saving the planet. Imagine if we started with the young and created awareness of planting and nurturing even just one tree, imagine the number of trees Earth could have then, he would hopefully wonder.

In the year 2020, Jadav was requested to collaborate with NGOs in Mexico. The goal was to plant more than seven million trees in an attempt to re-forest eight lakh hectares of land. Jadav was provided a ten-year visa by the Mexican government for the task in a project that would involve one lakh students per day.

The media may have given him much recognition but it were the trees that had first changed his whole life around. The jungle gave him a home, the ability to support a family and put food on his table. It was the jungle that took him across the seven seas. He went from the land where the sun rises first, to the land where it sets the last. And no matter where he was, his heart remained deeply rooted in the Molai forest, and he would carry it with him through all the lands he would wander…

6

PRINCE MANVENDRA SINGH GOHIL

Only Love Prevails

Manvendra Singh Gohil walked the stage while tens of thousands of people broke into a spirited applause. The year was 2008 and the place was the Euro Pride Gay Festival in Stockholm. The familiar rush of adrenaline coursed through his veins as he stepped out of the wings and met a crowd that was thrilled to see the exotically dressed Prince in his long coat, churidar, turban and jewels. And he had come all the way from India.

For Manvendra however, this was not a journey that could be measured in kilometres. It was an experience far more profound, a journey which had begun with him never having the courage to admit his truth to now, finally, proudly standing by it. It had taken forty-one years of his life to get here.

He took the mike in hand and saw the eager faces in the crowd ready to hear his story. And it was a story unlike others.

When Prince Manvendra Singh Gohil was born to Maharana Shri Raghubir Singhji Rajendra Singhji Sahib and Maharani Rukmini Devi in 1965, no one knew that the only male titular heir to the throne of the former princely state of Rajpipla would go on to write a very unique role for himself in the history of his family and his nation.

Located in the western part of Gujarat, Rajpipla was conquered by Muhideosur Guhil in the sixth century. Situated between the Narmada and Tapti rivers and bounded by the Satpura range of mountains in the South, this fertile land soon prospered under the Gohil Rajput dynasty. Over time, this tiny kingdom faced many invasions by the Sultans of Delhi as well as the Mughal emperors.

The 33rd Gohil ruler Maharana Verisalji II was one of the most prominent leaders of the 1857 revolt of independence against the British. To defend their land, the Gohils often resorted to guerilla warfare and other hit and run tactics. They were so successful that by the time the British became the sole rulers of India, Rajpipla was the second most important state after Baroda. And as the 39th direct descendant of the Gohil Rajput dynasty, a very conservative and equally revered one, Manvendra had large shoes to fill.

Born with a golden spoon in his mouth, his initial years were spent in the cocoon of the family palace in Rajpipla. He and his younger sister Princess Minaxi Kumari lacked nothing. Here, in the marble floored rooms and balconies, Manvendra spent hours playing with his little sister, their Governess, and countless other domestic helpers employed at the palace. The family was known for its lavish lifestyle. They employed more than a hundred helpers just in the royal kitchens. This was at a time when the King was considered a direct representative of God, and each one of the staff served the family with something akin to reverence.

Each room in the gigantic palace was a storehouse of priceless antiques, precious artifacts and rare animal skins. With the portraits of his ancestors watching over them,

Manvendra and Minaxi undertook many an adventure as only little children do. He had everything he could possibly want and was not 'allowed' to do even his own basic chores himself. If he so much as thought of getting a glass of water for himself, he was quickly reprimanded.

While Manvendra had everything, what he lacked was the attention of his parents. On the rare occasion that he did meet them, he was schooled in advance on how to behave before them. His conduct with them was expected to be very formal, all so he could be prepared for the public role he was to take on later in life. He addressed his parents by their titles, never with the affection of 'mummy' and 'papa'. As a result, the impressionable young boy grew up to believe that these visits were about meeting someone of eminence. He believed his Governess, the young lady who spent all her time with him and Minaxi were his mother. It was to them that he felt really close.

Manvendra had no friends while he was growing up, believed to be too high born to mix with the other children. The palace staff filled all the roles in his life whether that of friends or of family. But when it came to matters of importance in his life, the Maharana and the Maharani had the final say. When his parents found that Manvendra preferred using his left hand more than his right one, they were horrified. As the crown prince, he was already expected not just to grace a lot of social functions but also conduct a lot of religious ceremonies. And since all Hindu rituals are conducted with the right hand, Manvendra couldn't possibly be left-handed.

Immediate attempts to change his left-handedness were begun. The horrified Maharana even sent his son to doctors to get this habit fixed. These attempts confused Manvendra, making him wonder why he was being made to change what was natural and harmless to him. Fortunately, the doctors that were consulted all came to a unanimous conclusion that forcing Manvendra to use his right hand for writing and other tasks at this stage could cause mental issues. And so, for the time being, the matter was left alone.

At the time of independence, a total of 560 princely states had assimilated into a united nation called India. These princely states were given an annual allowance known as 'Privy Purse' as compensation for their efforts. In case the head of a princely state passed away, the allowance was then granted to his successor. In addition, the rulers of these princely states were also bestowed with some special privileges and the recognition of being the titular rulers. The Privy Purse however, was abolished in 1971 by the government of India. And with it went the allowances as well as the special privileges of its recipients.

Suddenly, all the royals of India were faced with new worries. Chief among them was how were they going to maintain their palaces and properties now, without any source of income? The royal families of India then began coming up with a unique solution, of turning their palaces into hotels and resorts. And Manvendra's parents too followed suit.

The six-year-old had no idea in 1971 that his life had changed forever. His parents, whose status was that of commoners now, decided to convert the family seat of Rajvant palace, built in 1915, into a resort. With his former home turning into a hotel, the Maharana took the decision to move the family to Mumbai. It was a big change for them but opulence and style was not for compromise even then. The Gohil family moved into a seven-bedroom mansion in Mumbai. There were about twenty-five servants in the house ready to do their bidding. Privilege was a word that was inseparable from Manvendra's life and people worshipped the ground he and his family walked on. They were treated with respect everywhere they went. A fact made obvious when at the tender age of ten, Manvendra was invited to be the chief guest at a school function.

In Mumbai, Manvendra and Minaxi were enrolled in the prestigious Bombay Scottish School and just like that, a new world opened up before him. Here in Bombay, he began to meet boys who were from different backgrounds, and it fascinated him. Because he had always been encouraged to keep a distance between himself and ordinary people, it was not the easiest for him to mix with people. His parents were busy with their own lives at these times of great changes. Their relationship with their son however continued with the same formality. All his day-to-day struggles were shared by his governess by his side.

Manvendra was ten when he realized that this woman who had raised him, who had been with him through all his challenging times and encouraged him all these years, was not his mother. She was paid to take care of him. On asking who his real mother was, he was told about the beautiful, regal and formal Maharani Rukmini Devi. It was a big blow to him. The realization was an eye opener. But like all young children, he tried to take it in his stride and move on.

The onset of puberty was a very strange time for Manvendra. The society he lived in considered it very normal for boys to like girls. And yet, he felt differently. While boys in his class were crushing over girls or their female teachers, Manvendra felt himself drawn towards men, specifically his male teachers. His young heart yearned to tell someone about the way he felt but he was also too scared to do so.

He soon began to realise that he was different. To add to his woes, homosexuality was a matter so hushed in the India of 1977, that there was no book or person to explain his own feelings to him. When he looked around in his home, he thought it very normal for men to share close relationships. Especially in a set-up where men and women lived in segregated quarters called *Mardana* and the *Zenana*. Even the male helpers who looked after him did so with deep rooted love and affection.

To a young Manvendra, everything was confusing. He felt lonely, like he was harbouring a great secret that he could tell no one for fear of ridicule. And by the time he turned twelve years old, he knew for sure that he was not like other boys.

Often the thought of telling his parents would come to him and he would often wonder how he would broach this subject with them. He didn't even know if there was anyone else like him, or if he was the only one who felt like this. With so many people surrounding him, ready to concede to his every demand and cater his every whim, he still felt very alone.

By the time he had finished with his education, it became harder to deny his true self. Manvendra finally decided that he would have to tell his parents. And when he did muster the courage to tell them, he was faced by an outright denial of who he was. They refused to even consider that such a thing could be true about their son. They tried to convince him that it was he who was mistaken. But after Manvendra repeatedly asserted that he was not confused, his stricken mother began to look for ways to 'de-homosexualise' him.

Appointments were sought with some of the most prominent doctors, and on conditions of anonymity, they were urged to make Manvendra 'normal' again. For the already confused prince, guilt too was now added to his sense of shame for liking men. However, the conclusion of all the doctors was that these attempts to change Manvendra's orientation would not do him any good and would affect him mentally. But even the law did not support men like Manvendra, back when homosexuality was still a criminal offense.

Maharani Rukmini Devi was already reeling from the revelation that her firstborn and heir to the family lineage liked men. And since the doctors couldn't do anything, in her frenzy she turned to the only recourse left to her—getting Manvendra married. Desperate to make his parents happy and to fit in, he too agreed for marriage, hoping that it would make everything normal. He prayed for the day when he would have children. He could then live like all the other men he saw around him.

Feelers were sent out and various eligible young women from royal lineages were short-listed. Manvendra was drawn to a beautiful princess from the state of Jhabua in Madhya Pradesh. He indicated his preference to his parents and wished to get to know her better before they tied the knot. As soon as he said he liked the Princess, the marriage date was set. A hasty but lavish royal wedding followed. The young princess, nursing dreams of a wonderful life, entered Manvendra's life. No one was more relieved to see Manvendra married and settled than his parents. The Maharana and Maharani were sure that all these newfangled ideas he had of liking men were a nightmare that could now be relegated to the past.

Manvendra on the other hand tried his best to make things normal. But he could not make himself love the princess. She, on the other hand, couldn't understand why despite having it all, there was something amiss in their marriage. The princess finally realized that neither she nor her husband was happy together, so there was no point in carrying on the sham. It was a heart-breaking time for them since their relationship did not just involve them but the reputations of both their families. When she made her decision known to Manvendra, his feelings of guilt and misery were compounded manifold. Now, he had pulled another human being into this mess, and she was being punished for no fault of her own.

Manvendra's parents too were left dismayed. They could not allow this to happen. But nothing could be done and in a span of fifteen months of his marriage, prince Manvendra found himself divorced. A failed marriage of the scion of the Gohil Rajput dynasty was a scandal in the royal circles. To Manvendra this was not a concern. He was bruised by all the negativity and hurt that had been afflicted on the woman he had married and divorced, all of it an outcome of his inability to own up the truth—his truth.

He began to question himself. With the breakdown of Manvendra's marriage, the family received more proposals for a prospective bride. How many more people would have to go through the same thing, Manvendra asked himself. He refused to think of marriage. If anything, Manvendra was more certain that he was gay.

Unable to accept the turn of events, the Maharani and Maharana now amped up their efforts to 'cure' Manvendra of this malady. More doctors were consulted. The Maharani insisted Manvendra be given shock therapy—a treatment involving jolts of current passed through the brain. The currents are supposed to cause a change in brain chemistry that can reverse certain symptoms of health conditions. When the shock therapy did not give the desired results, Maharani Rukmini Devi wanted Manvendra to undergo surgery in his brain to alter his orientation.

Manvendra was subjected to numerous treatments. Eventually even the doctors refused to carry them out. They all came to the same conclusion: this was not a physical or mental illness that could be cured. They told his parents that one's sexual orientation is not something that can be changed, one is born with it. They declared that they could spend all the money they wanted on trying to change the way Manvendra felt, but it wouldn't amount to anything.

His parents refused to believe that their son, with such impeccable cultural upbringing, could be gay. They did not see that while Manvendra did indeed have a very good upbringing, it could have no relation to his sexuality.

When the Doctors had given up again, his parents insisted he meet with spiritual guides and religious leaders. Manvendra subjected himself to all of it. He was in a nightmare that he wasn't sure he would get out of with his sanity intact. And if he had hoped for a cure from these visits, he didn't find any. What was worse was the feeling of terrible guilt he was left with about the kind of man he was. Slowly and steadily he began to wonder if ending his life was the only way out…

But fate had other plans. Just when he felt absolutely worthless, he happened to cross paths with Ashok Row Kavi. Ashok is a journalist with a career that spanned almost two decades. After working in several magazines and newspapers, Ashok started India's first magazine for gay men called *Bombay Dost*. Seeing the young prince in such a disheartened state stirred Ashok enough to begin to mentor him.

Ashok was a godsend in Manvendra's life. He taught him more about himself than Manvendra could have hoped to ever learn. Ashok made him believe that he was not an aberration of nature, helping him redeem of the guilt that had become an intrinsic part of him. He told him that there were many more people like him across the world. Most importantly, Ashok explained to Manvendra how he could never change the way he felt. And that he didn't need to.

Ashok instilled a sense of pride in Manvendra. It was a new feeling for him. There was slowly a huge shift in the way Manvendra viewed himself. Before the world could accept him, he would have to accept himself. He was a man who liked men. And slowly that was becoming okay. Along with pride finally followed the acceptance that his orientation was something he was born with, not something a doctor or a spiritual Guru could fix.

He began to feel inspired by the roads his mentor had guided him through. And soon he started his own non-profit organization called Lakshya. It was made with the aim of improving the rights of the LGBTQ in the state of Gujarat. In an ironic turn of events, he received financial support for Lakshya from the most unexpected quarters—the government.

One ripple at a time, Manvendra went through a sea of change in his outlook. From thinking he was a liability, he started believing that he had it in him to give back to society. While his own family was not ready to face the truth about him as yet, the world was another matter. Despite the best efforts of Maharani Rukmini Devi to keep his sexual orientation a secret, he knew things couldn't stay the same.

Manvendra and his family left Mumbai and came back to Rajpipla, the place where they felt completely at home. He was now actively involved with activities of Lakshya. But he knew that he was not being entirely honest as yet.

For him to be confident in the world, he would have to own up to his truth. And he did so by giving an interview to a Gujarati newspaper in the year 2006. The story was about the only gay prince of India, who had finally chosen to come out publically. It was the first-time royalty had exposed itself this way. And it was an attempt that deserved praise. However, when the interview was published, it was something akin to an earthquake that shook Rajpipla, then all of Gujarat, to become the talk of all of India.

This interview single-handedly changed a lot of things. For starters, the people of Rajpipla were shocked and then immensely angry. They came out in large numbers to protest the publication of the interview. Effigies of the prince were burnt on the roads. The public turned its ire on to the royal family, particularly the prince. Letters with death threats made their way to him. The royal family was so angry with the prince that his parents refused to speak to him. Even a lot of his gay friends deserted him, scared that they would be exposed by their association with him.

The very people who had treated him like God were after his blood now.

At this time, alone and without any support, the prince should have felt even more hopeless. But he felt reborn. He could finally be himself before the world. And it was the most unfettered he had felt his entire life.

As freeing as it tends to be though, the truth can also lead you to the loneliest of places. This the prince found out with each passing day. Isolated by family and denied by friends, there was not much Manvendra could do about his situation. His own mother had a very hard time accepting the truth. She disowned him. And to legitimize this, she released advertisements in the paper that said Manvendra was no longer a part of her family. He was asked to vacate the royal premises. And she threatened to take to court anyone who referred to Manvendra as her son.

He was paying a very heavy price for speaking the truth. To make matters worse, one day a summon arrived for him from the Dowager Maharani, his paternal grandmother. As he presented himself in the royal apartments of the formidable figure of Dowager Maharani, Manvendra braced himself for the worst. To his utmost shock however, the Maharani greeted him with a hug. She told him that she was happy for him. For someone who was hanging on to his sanity by a thread, this was more than Manvendra could ask for. His tears poured unchecked, in joy and relief. And his grandma comforted him, trying to erase some of the sadness her grandson was going through for no fault of his own.

With Rajpipla still outraged many days after the news broke out, support from unexpected quarters soon lifted

up Manvendra's spirits more. It was a letter sent by the Senior Citizens Association of Rajpipla. They expressed not just their support but admiration for him. He was slowly beginning to feel that all these years of hiding the truth were worth nothing. He should have done this sooner. Even his now ninety-seven-year-old, retired secretary got in touch with him, asking Manvendra if he could show his support by marching with him.

Hope arrived from another corner in his life, in the form of Prince Amar Singh from the royal family of Kapurthala. Amar Singh publicly stood by Manvendra when he was being vilified. He offered to work for the LGBTQ rights in India and received threats for his efforts but nothing could waver him. Manvendra on his part continued to stand by his belief that the people were not to be blamed, only their ignorance.

He was still trying to grapple with his changed circumstances when he received an invitation from the world-famous talk show host, Oprah Winfrey, to come and share his story. He was the second Indian she had ever invited. Manvendra knew that the only way to deal with the issue was head-on and this was his chance to do exactly that. He accepted the invitation and appeared on her show and talked about how with his truth and his story out in the world had made him an outcast for many, a hero to few.

His sincerity and humour endeared him not just to the audience, but also Oprah. Prince Manvendra became the only Indian to be invited to the Oprah show thrice. With his story reaching millions of people around the globe, the world could now not get enough of him. From meeting politicians to Hollywood celebrities to inaugurating and giving talks at

Pride festivals that celebrate the LGBTQ community, he saw it all.

In his efforts towards getting Section 377 repealed, Manvendra took the help of Justice Michael Kirby from Australia, the first judge of the Australian court to openly come out as gay. Here, Justice Kirby met a number of politicians, judges and lawyers. He listened to their point of view but expressed his own views too in pushing for the abolishment of Section 377. This was a very big step in the long fight for the freedom to love.

A few years later, in 2013, Manvendra got married for the second time to an American, De Andre Richardson. There was no confusion in his mind this time, no guilt that he was doing deep injustice to the person he was marrying. This decision alone made a world of a difference to Manvendra. De Andre proved to be the man Manvendra needed to push him out of his comfort zone and do the things he had really wanted to do. He had a dream of establishing a refuge for LGBTQ couples who were ostracized by society because of their orientation which now looked like a real possibility, as he began looking for places he could set up such a shelter.

In 2017, Manvendra was invited to be a part of a few episodes of the show *Keeping Up With The Kardashians.* And now, he became a household name. But the sweetest victory was when he came back home and became a celebrity among his younger cousins. The very people who had deserted him when he had admitted to being gay were now queuing up to take a selfie with him. Manvendra had never forgotten his values and chose to be humble even in victory.

Over time, even the disharmony with Manvendra's parents dissolved. As a way to make up for all that Manvendra had been put through, he was given the royal palace of Hanumanteshwar.

But nothing could compare to the way Manvendra felt on the 6th of September 2018 when the Supreme Court decriminalized Section 377. The religious leaders of India had united to fight against the ruling but the tireless efforts of people like Manvendra culminated in victory. But there was no time to rest. He immediately knew what he had to do next.

The royal palace, where he was once thrown out of was now the place where he finally realized his dream. In the sprawling fifteen acres of the palace grounds, he established the shelter for LGBTQ people. Manvendra knew that the battle was not over. But for now, he had taken another step in the right direction. This was just the beginning. The prince born with a golden spoon had found a way to transform and enrich the lives of others.

7
MAJOR SANDEEP UNNIKRISHNAN

Duty before Self

"Don't come up, I will handle them," the team members of the most elite fighting force in the country heard Major Sandeep Unnikrishnan say, as he decided to proceed with the mission alone. The fateful day was 27th November 2008. The Major had taken the decision to prevent any more damage to the lives of his team members.

Later, as Shri K. Unnikirshan would grieve over his son's life and death, he would say that had Sandeep survived and come home, he would have got a scolding for going on such a dangerous mission alone. And Sandeep would have said to him, like he always did, "Appa, life is for dying on the line of duty."

But even through the sorrow and tears, he knew it would have been futile to caution his then thirty-one-year-old son. Because he had always known Sandeep for having the instinct of protecting others, before a care for his own self. Maybe that is why his parents never wanted him to be in the Army. Whenever Dhanalakshmi, his mother, stated her opposition to Sandeep's wish of joining the armed forces, he only had one argument. He would ask her, if every mother thought the way she did, then who would think about the motherland? That was the clincher every time. And his wish was granted.

Not only did Sandeep live to protect his country, but he laid down his life for it too.

On the 26th of November in 2008, Major Sandeep Unnikrishnan died guarding the lives of civilians from one of the worst terrorist attacks ever orchestrated in India. While the perpetrators were subdued everywhere else in Mumbai, at three places the battle raged on. One of the sites was the hundred-year-old Taj Mahal Palace and Tower Hotel.

Five hours after the attack, when the hotel was still under siege, the government decided to bring in the 51 Special Action Group (SAG)—experts in counter-terrorism operations and stealth warfare, also known as the Black Cats. They are the most dangerous warriors of the Indian Army. And Sandeep was one of the finest training officers of this lethal group.

As a training officer, there was no requirement for him to be present for the mission. But when he heard about the attack, he immediately volunteered to be a part of Operation Black Tornado, launched against the attackers hiding in the Taj Mahal Palace. When the 51 SAG arrived in Mumbai, it wasted no time in launching the operation. And a host of problems awaited them.

The terrorists as part of their plan had the advantage of detailed maps of the hotel. With the arrival of the Black Cat Commandos, the operation that was being handled by the Marine Commandos (MARCOS) and the Mumbai police was handed over to the 51 SAG But there were no maps available of the hotel. The hotel staff could not establish any contact with the architect either. This meant that like the

Mumbai police and the MARCOS, the 51 SAG would have to operate blind.

The terrorists on the other hand had managed to locate the room that contained all the CCTV camera feed and destroyed it. This meant that no one could now figure out what was going on in any part of the hotel. They had split up into groups so they could control different parts of the hotel and lay traps for the commandos.

The entire hotel beyond the lobby was now full of concealed traps like trip wires which set off bombs and innocent civilians who were gagged and hooked to bombs which went off the minute the commandos tried to free them. Many civilians were taken hostage as both an easy target and a valuable asset for negotiation. The terrorists had put on the uniform of the dead hotel staff or of the police so they could fool the commandos as well as the civilians.

Launching a multi-level attack was not possible for the SAG The commandos could not use radio communication during the operation because the terrorists could easily tune in to the frequency of their walkie-talkies. The use of any kind of weapon like tear gas was not possible since the civilians were also involved. And the worst nightmare for the commandos was the presence of countless media persons outside the Taj who were hell bent on relaying all the minute details of the operation so nothing the SAG did could be done discreetly. With their eyes and hands figuratively tied, the SAG sent snipers to surround the hotel from the outside. All vantage points were covered so that the minute a terrorist came into view from the outside, he could be put down. Sandeep now proceeded with his team of ten commandos into the hotel.

They would have to comb all the five floors with seventy-five rooms each, from door to door, until all the terrorists were killed and each hostage rescued.

This was the operation that Sandeep was leading his men into. As the head of the operation, when two of his commandos were injured during fire from the terrorists, he arranged for their evacuation and at the same time engaged with the terrorists' firing guns. In the process, he managed to rescue a number of civilians along with his team. Clearing the guests of the hotel from floor to floor was no easy task. Many had already met death on the other side of the door. They answered thinking it was the NSG come to help. That's how they tricked them. Death was their only fate.

Sandeep and the SAG tirelessly went to each room, assuaging the frayed nerves of those rescued, leading the guests to safety while holding off fire from the terrorists. Besides, the building was a burning inferno with the grenades being constantly lobbed in different parts of the hotel. Thousands of litres of water had been poured into the place to douse the raging fires. As a result, the carpets on all the floors were wet and squelched. Moving stealthily was impossible.

After more than fifteen hours of evacuation, the only way to get to the terrorists was through the iconic grand central staircase of the hotel. Sandeep and his team pursued their target only to realise that the terrorists were trying to get away. It was here that he made the decision of pursuing them alone.

He went after the four hardened terrorists, cornered them in the Ballroom of the northern end of the hotel. In this fight of one against four, Sandeep did not lose courage. This time the terrorists had more than met their match. The lone warrior kept fighting back, instilling fear in those who had dared to attack innocent, unarmed people. But to achieve his aim, he had to make the ultimate sacrifice.

The ill-fated day was the 26th of November in 2011. The people targeted were the residents of Mumbai. But the message was for the whole nation. Terrorists and Pakistani extremists would not rest in peace nor let anyone else be in peace until India bled through a thousand cuts. Mumbai being the financial centre of India was on the hit list.

The perpetrators were a group of ten gunmen. They had been trained to kill mercilessly, destroy recklessly and cause maximum chaos by the Lashkar-e-Taiba, a terrorist organization based in Pakistan. The assailants had trained there, then boarded a cargo ship from Pakistan and sailed for Indian waters where they hijacked an Indian fishing boat and killed all the crew on board. That's how they made their way to the coast of Mumbai. Once here, they used inflatable boats to reach closer to the Gateway of India where they alighted and broke up into groups. From there they proceeded to their targets, places that were heavily populated and would result in maximum deaths.

Their targets were the innocent civilians at Chhatrapati Shivaji railway station, the Jewish Centre, Leopold café, a movie theatre, two hospitals and two luxury hotels. The attacks left in their wake a death toll of 175 people. This included civilians, foreigners, children, security personnel and nine of the ten attackers. While the Mumbai police and security personnel were caught off-guard by the unprecedented attacks, they managed to deal with the terrorists quickly. But the longest siege was at the Taj Mahal Palace and Tower

Hotel. Stuck in that gruesome chaos was Sandeep, a soldier who made the choice to fight and sacrifice his life.

His story begins thirty-one years ago on the 15th of March 1977. Sandeep was born to K. Unnikrishnan Nair and Dhanalakshmi in Cheruvannar in Kerala. From a young age, Sandeep had the instinct to put others before self. He was nurturing the dream ever since he was a child and would wait year round to go see the Navy Day parades with his father.

A diligent, humble student, Sandeep was at the Frank Anthony Public School, Bangalore for fourteen years and enjoyed sports and photography. Sporting a crew cut, a variant of the military style, he was a favourite of everyone in school and of the girls in particular. An instance that the family often recalled about the polite, young man being oblivious to his popularity was the time when he and his father came back home to find more than a dozen pair of shoes lined outside the door. They entered only to see Dhanalakshmi crowded by many girls trying to convince her that they would be the perfect fit for Sandeep. It was in response to a rumour doing rounds at school that Dhanalakshmi wanted to get Sandeep married!

After graduating in 1995 with a Bachelor's Degree in Science, Sandeep wanted to join the Indian Navy. He sat for the Navy entrance exams while his parents thought he was training to be a doctor. But he failed the medical test due to his eyesight. His parents were relieved and wrongly assumed that his obsession to join the armed forces would recede. But Sandeep already had his next strategy planned. He sat for the entrance test of the Indian Army and cleared it. When his parents asked him why he was so intent on joining the Army, he simply said that no one else can ever get the respect a soldier does. A profound realization struck them right then. Sandeep was never really theirs to begin with. His heart always beat for the nation.

Despite his parents' disapproval, Sandeep joined the National Defense Academy and they had to go along with his decisions. Here he was a part of the Oscar Squadron, a group of about 120 officers who lived together in one block. Students from this squadron had even gone on to represent the country in Olympics. His discipline and hard work ensured that he was soon excelling in academics. But it was his humility and generosity that made him so well liked.

After graduating as part of the 94th course of NDA, Sandeep joined the Indian Military Academy course in Dehradun. Here again, he distinguished himself as a cadet who was outstanding, brilliant, and full of humility. He passed out in 1999 leaving a distinct imprint on the hearts of all those he studied with. From here he was commissioned as lieutenant into the 7th Battalion of Bihar Regiment in 1999. He was all of twenty-two years old then.

At the 7th Battalion Sandeep learnt how to hone his skills on ground. Here he was with a regiment known for disciplined soldiers who were capable of applying with enthusiasm the tactical drills that were taught to them. Sandeep soon learnt it was only his courage against all odds that made him different, that made him a soldier. His life, and even death, a testimony, Sandeep would not shy away from putting this lesson into practice time and again.

Sandeep considered it a matter of pride when he was included in Operation Vijay of the Kargil War in 1999.

Pakistani troops, disguised as Indian Kashmiri militants, entered the Indian side of the Line of Control and captured strategic positions. The aim of the operation was to flush out the militants, at great risk to their lives. The Indian Army, with support from the Air Force, managed to re-capture a majority of the positions on the Indian side.

Sandeep was deployed at the forward post in this operation, a position where his Battalion faced heavy artillery shelling from Pakistani troops. However, despite the imminent danger, on the evening of 31st December, in the face of heavy firing and shelling, Sandeep led a team of six soldiers and managed to reclaim lost territory and established a post of the Indian Army. The post was just two-hundred metres away from the Pakistani one!

Promotions came in quick succession to this braveheart. In 2003, Sandeep was promoted to the rank of Captain and in 2005, he was made a Major. Despite the tough life he led, often through situations where his life was threatened by the possibility of death, Sandeep thanked his luck for being able to serve the country. A majority of his salary quietly went into helping out others, a fact that became known to his parents only after his passing. He would donate to a number of charitable institutions. He even bore the total health expense of the mother of a colleague. Not known to all, Sandeep's bravery was also marked by the wont to take care of others.

He went on to train at the High Altitude Warfare School at Gulmarg, learning counter intelligence and survival skills. He would serve three postings in Kashmir, even serving at the Siachen glacier, the place that has the reputation of being one of the world's most dangerous battlefields. He was also posted in Gujarat and Rajasthan after which he was selected to join the National Security Guard, a very coveted offer.

Sandeep accepted it without any hesitation and proved to be so good that he was selected to be a trainer with the Black Cats on the completion of his course. He was appointed as the trainer for 51 SAG Even here, Sandeep proved to be the best trainer that they had seen—a no-nonsense officer and yet a loving superior who was never impolite to anyone.

On the 26th of November in 2008, when the Mumbai terror attacks began, Sandeep was serving the 51 SAG as a trainer in Manesar. When the decision to deploy the NSG was conveyed to Sandeep and his team, Sandeep immediately volunteered. As a trainer, he was not meant to go on field operations. And as the best instructor the SAG had seen in a long time, his seniors were not willing to let him go. But Sandeep would not take no for an answer. His defense was that if he really was that good, he needed to be where his team was, fighting back the miscreants who had dared to invade his country. It could prove to be fatal; he was taking a chance on his life. But he was ready for the gamble—the final act of heroism that won him the hearts of millions.

8

PANDIT BHIMSEN JOSHI

The Voice of God

Pandit Bhimsen Joshi was distressed. Great men too are troubled by the small inconveniences of life. He tried to turn on the ignition of his beloved car for the hundredth time and the engine did not purr to life. He could not afford to waste any more time, he concluded. As he got out of the car, his friend Shrikant Deshpande wondered if they would ever make it to the venue on time, if at all. "We must look for a mechanic now. We have lost enough time in trying to fix the car," he ventured to Pandit-ji. "Hmm..." mumbled Pandit-ji as he began to walk ahead.

Shrikant was doubtful if they would find a mechanic on this road though. They were on their way from the small pilgrimage town of Pandharpur to Nagpur to perform at a classical musical recital. An audience awaited a glimpse of the musical genius, to hear the voice, which was said, would be the voice of God, if He ever sang. Since Pandit-ji loved cars second only to music, he had decided to drive the distance, more than five-hundred-kilometres, by himself. His friend and fellow disciple Shrikant was also accompanying him on the road trip. They had been cruising along when the car suddenly came to a halt in the middle of their journey, on a long, deserted stretch of the road. This was more than an hour ago, and not a soul had passed this way since.

But when Shrikant saw what Pandit-ji was walking towards, his sagging spirits rose instantly. There, at a great distance, was a lone man, a farmer from the looks of it, riding a cycle in their direction. As Pandit-ji walked towards him, Shrikant settled back into the car. Pandit-ji would probably ask the man to go and get a mechanic to fix the car, he thought, and they could finally be on their way.

Shrikant allowed himself to close his eyes for a short nap; after all it would be a while before the mechanic would appear. But in seconds he was awakened by the sound of a tap on the car window. He looked out to see Pandit-ji standing with a cycle, gesturing him to step out. A few minutes later, Shrikant found himself riding the cycle that Pandit-ji had borrowed from the farmer. Riding pillion was Pandit-ji, who was now practicing a *raag*. "But I don't understand, Pandit-ji," interrupted Shrikant. "Weren't you asking the farmer to go and get the mechanic? Where are we going to find him?"

"Oh, did I forget to mention? We aren't going to look for the mechanic. The farmer will do that. I thought instead of wasting time, we should directly head to the concert venue in Nagpur. The car will reach us there!" said Pandit-ji nonchalantly, resuming his practice. Shrikant took a deep breath as he prepared himself for the long, arduous journey that lay ahead. He marvelled at the dedication of Pandit-ji, middle-aged and spirited, refusing to let a broken-down car get in the way of his performance. They reached the venue in time for Pandit-ji to perform before the huge crowd and ride the complicated crests and dips of the song he sang so effortlessly. Shrikant, like the rest of the audience, watched him in awe, impressed by the immensity of his talent but unsurprised by his eccentricities.

He had heard stories of how a young Pandit-ji often bicycled to venues from Pune to Phaltan to perform. Along with him would ride as his sidekick, the famed harmonium player, Appa Jalgaonkar with his harmonium in tow. The roads would be bumpy, and the sun would scorch them. By the time they reached the venue, Appa, exhausted, would barely be able to walk but Pandit-ji would perform for seven or even eight hours without so much as a hint of fatigue. If anything, he seemed more energised. Even now, Shrikant could sense a fire coursing through him, as he mesmerised his audience with an old Raag performed in a fresh way. He felt blessed to be able to witness the maestro in his glory.

There was only one word to describe Pandit-ji's present state—ecstatic.

He had always been like this, the happiest when he could sing, even when there was no one listening. Even when he was alone, hungry and tired and far away from everyone he loved, it was music that was his sole companion.

If music coursed through his veins today, it was because in embracing it, Pandit Bhimsen Joshi had truly given up everything he had. Music was what he was born for, the only thing he couldn't live without, and the destiny he began reaching out for even before he could learn what the word meant.

His grandfather was a respected *Kirtankar*, who sang devotional songs. So, when Bhimsen Gururaj Joshi came into the world on 4th of February 1922 in the sleepy village of

Gadag in Karnataka, he had already been exposed to music as a means of devotion to God by the voice of his grandfather. Then, it was only a matter of time for Bhimsen to begin singing too. Listening to his mother hum devotional songs, often to the tune of Tanpura that she played herself, Bhimsen began to sing along with her. Not just singing but with many musical instruments strewn around the house, he learnt to also play the Harmonium and Tanpura.

Music enchanted him. The more he looked for it, the more he found it everywhere, in all walks of life, in everything he did. He was bewitched by the melodious voices of the muezzins calling the faithful to pray in their village every evening. The only thing left to do then was to chase it.

If a procession of singers was passing by their house, singing *Abhangs* in praise of God, the young Bhimsen would discreetly set out following the procession and join in the singing. He would follow them wherever they went, losing all sense of time, forgetting that he ought to go back home. Bhimsen's increasing zest for music was slowly becoming a nuisance for his family. Gururaj would often come back tired after a long day only to be told that Bhimsen was missing again. Dropping everything, he would step out into the darkness, lantern in hand to look for his firstborn. He would often find him far away from home. On days when he was unable to trace his son, Gururaj would ask for the assistance of the police. Bhimsen would be brought back while being given an earful on how he should not wander away like this since any danger could befall him. He would even instruct his wife to hide any musical instrument from Bhimsen so he would not get his hands on them.

But for someone who found music in the rustling of leaves, the twittering of birds, in the gusts of wind and falling rain, his father's words were hard to follow. When Gururaj finally accepted that it was impossible to stop his nine-year-old son from getting lost in these musical processions, he came up with the perfect solution. With his own hand, Gururaj wrote 'Son of Teacher Joshi' on the shirts Bhimsen wore. This ensured that no matter where Bhimsen strayed, he was brought back to the right address. Life for Bhimsen was a melody he could enjoy with the love of his parents protecting him. But it was not going to remain so for long.

Gururaj was not very happy about Bhimsen leaning towards music. A revered teacher and academic, who had authored the much valued Kannada to English dictionary, it was only natural that he hoped his son should follow suit and secure his future.

But fate had other things in store for Bhimsen. Tragedy soon struck and his mother passed away. With that loving hand and saintly presence gone from his life forever, Bhimsen felt adrift. It was at this time that music became his refuge from grief.

Life moved on and his father eventually remarried. Being the oldest of the sixteen siblings, Bhimsen was met by high expectations from the family. His father wanted him to take up Engineering or Medicine as a profession, but Bhimsen found it impossible to ignore music and would instead neglect his studies. Gururaj would often hear that Bhimsen had not turned up at school because he got distracted by one thing or the other, which always had something to do with music. Bhimsen on his part did not like to constantly be held accountable for his studies by his father.

Time went by but the contention over Bhimsen's future remained a source of unrest between the father and son. And another constant that remained to play out was Bhimsen's love for melody. He would still find it everywhere and was beginning to realise that dedicating his life to making music was what he really wanted to do. It was also the time when classical music was flourishing in Karnataka. Home to musicians from the Carnatic as well as the Hindustani streams, for a curious mind, it was a treasure trove. Bhimsen would often hear different artists performing, whether live or on records, and he would try to imitate their style of singing.

One day, as he was walking to school, he heard "the voice". It was playing in a shop wanting to grab attention in the marketplace. "*Piyabinaaaotnaahi chain*," sang the voice of Ustad Abdul Karim Khan who had founded the Kirana Gharana of music. A Gharana is a community or group of performers who have a musical style that is distinct from other styles. It can often be traced to originating from a particular region. Ustad Abdul Karim Khan was from the small village of Kirana and later went on to become the court singer in the royal court of Baroda.

Khan Sahab was singing the Raag Basant. And the eleven-year-old Bhimsen was suddenly transported away from the hot, dusty road he was standing on to a moment of serenity in a beautiful green garden on a cool spring evening. And the voice of Khan Sahab was wafting softly in the wind like the perfume of the flowers. This was the place Bhimsen wanted to be in. It was then he knew things would never be the same again. His fate was sealed. It seemed to him that the heavens had parted and revealed his life's purpose. From that day on,

Bhimsen had only one question in his heart, "What does one have to do to be able to sing like that?"

It was a thought he became obsessed with. He would try to imitate Ustad Abdul Karim Khan's style which was based on the Khayal Gayaki style of singing. It was a continuous-paced style of singing based on the Ragas. He was back from the dream of the garden, but it was the only place he wanted to go back to. He was consumed by the question. If only he could train with Hafiz Ali Khan Sahab who imparted training in Khayal Gayaki…

One balmy evening at dinner, Bhimsen sat with the rest of his family and ate his meal. Not content with the amount of ghee that was served to him, he asked for more. Since giving extra ghee to one child would mean giving more to all the rest, his step-mother refused. It wasn't a luxury they could afford. But earnest and callow, her refusal was immensely upsetting to the young man. He left his meal uneaten and his mind made up.

The following day, he left home for school as if nothing was wrong. But instead of reaching school, Bhimsen found his way to the Gadag railway station. With no money to buy a ticket, the young boy in a creased shirt and half pants boarded a train to Gwalior, the place where Khayal Gayaki style originated. He had no money, no plan on how to reach his destination and no one to turn to. But the one thing he did have that refused to let fear govern him was his dream. And like all dreamers, he wasn't afraid to take on the world.

The train journey though came with its own set of concerns. Bhimsen was worried about the Ticket Collector.

"How would I explain my ticketless state to him?" he wondered, until he decided it would be best to try his luck and be honest than waste time making up stories. And so, when the TC came around and asked him for a ticket, all he had to say was that he didn't have one because he had run away from his home to pursue classical singing. The TC had over the long course of his career come across many dishonest adults. This was the first time a young boy was trying to pull a fast one on him. And he wasn't about to let him go that easily.

"You ran away from home to learn singing? All right, sing us a few lines so we can decide for ourselves if you even have the talent for it or not," said the TC. The people around them nodded in agreement. A connoisseur of classical music himself, the TC knew that as soon as this little boy sang his piece, he would be brutally honest with him and send him packing home.

Bhimsen cleared his throat nervously. He was asked to perform and though nerves wracked him, he refused to engage his fear. He had taken the first step; there was no other way but to go ahead. Bhimsen began to sing, a bit unsure at first but as the seconds passed by, he no longer stood in the moving train. He was sitting in a lush green garden, and music was his only companion. He sang with abandon, free of all worries, only enjoying the moment.

Five minutes later, when he opened his eyes, he was back in the train. But this time there was something about the way everyone looked at him that made him uneasy. He waited for a reaction. The silence was broken by the rhythm of the train running over the tracks. Bhimsen finally cleared his throat.

The TC was the first one to speak. "Aahaa! That was a song by Panditrao Nagarkar Narayanrao Vyasji. You did good boy. Now what did you say your name was?" Bhimsen allowed himself a smile before he answered, "I didn't, Sahab. My name is Bhimsen Joshi." The TC nodded and then said, "You know what? You should go and learn. I can only let you travel for four more stations from here. From then on, it's your luck. Who knows, you might meet another fan of classical music like me!"

As the TC walked away, Bhimsen was thrilled. If he could convince one TC, who knew what other miraculous possibilities lay before him. Even his co-passengers showed less animosity towards him once the TC sanctioned his ticketless travel. Bhimsen sat down gingerly in the corner of a seat. This was a sign. He couldn't help but feel that good things were in store for him. His spontaneous step out from the comfort of his home into the great unknown wouldn't be so bad after all.

However, not everyone could be convinced through the notes of a song. Bhimsen learnt this the hard way when he found himself in jail the very next day. The TC on the next route was not amused by Bhimsen's music and on finding that he was ticketless; he did what he did with all such passengers—sent him to jail. And so, alone in his cell, Bhimsen realized something very important. No, it wasn't that he needed to go back home. What he needed was some money to avoid going to jail.

No sooner was Bhimsen out that he hopped right back on to the next train to Bijapur. But this time, before the TC arrived, he performed before the crowds and managed to make some money that would help him in reaching his destination. Still Bhimsen ended up in jail a few times. He also got to ride ticketless several times. By the end of two months, Bhimsen disembarked at Gwalior, a big centre for Hindustani classical music.

The distraught parents of Bhimsen had lodged a missing person police complaint for him by then, and Bhimsen was just getting started. He had also decided what his next step was going to be. He made his way to the residence of Hafiz Ali Khan Sahab, the court musician in Gwalior. While Khan Sahab played the Sarod, a stringed instrument used popularly in Hindustani music, he was also known for the Khayal style of singing. So, Bhimsen presented himself before the great musician and said that he wanted to become his student. He honestly admitted that while he did not have the money to pay as fee, he could do odd jobs to earn his keep.

It was not usual for Khan Sahab to be approached by runaway young children who had a burning desire to learn. What Khan Sahab did next was something Bhimsen would owe him for life. Khan Sahab who was under the patronage of the Maharaja of Gwalior got Bhimsen admitted into the Madhav Sangeet Vidyalaya, considered a leading centre for training in the Khayal style of singing in those days.

It was at this school that he was taught all the technical aspects of the Khayal form of singing. He was finally on the road to his destination. So enthusiastic was Bhimsen about learning that he absorbed everything like a sponge, especially the Raag Marwa and Raag Puriya. Within no time, he began to get restless again. He felt like there was more he could learn. And the only person he thought could teach him more was Hafiz Ali Khan Sahab.

Bhimsen managed to directly approach Khan Sahab once more and requested him to teach him the intricacies of the Khayal Gayaki, specifically his two favourite Raags, Marwa and Puriya. Khan Sahab agreed and began to teach this determined young boy. Bhimsen on his part proved to be the perfect student. His evenings were spent at Khan Sahab's residence learning, absorbing and practicing all he could.

Life was beginning to follow a predictable path but soon the direction to this path was going to be altered. Since Khan Sahab was famous and had to travel to several places for performing, his stays in Gwalior were few and far between. Bhimsen realized that he would have to do something about it.

One of the teachers at the Madhav Sangeet Vidyalaya mentioned to him that Bhishmadev Chatterjee of Kolkata was another leading singer who had mastered the Raag Gandhar, apart from the many other accomplished singers who resided in the city. After much thought, and driven by the temptation to perfect his craft, Bhimsen finally decided to leave Gwalior and head to Kolkata.

Thus began the next chapter of Bhimsen's quest for finding a Guru. He reached Kolkata and began to look for a way to meet Bhishmadev Chatterjee. In the process, he met Pahari Sanyal, a famous Bengali actor who was also a very good classical singer. Sure that there was a lot he could learn from him, Bhimsen immediately volunteered when he found out Pahari was looking for a servant. And that is how Bhimsen began to live in the home of the actor who would be out of the house for shoots all the time. 'Joshi' as he was called by Pahari, would spend his day doing household chores. Since he often sang for movies, the evenings at Pahari Sanyal's home would be filled with song rehearsals.

In between being asked to serve the guests, Bhimsen would sit in the song rehearsals. He would often receive a great tip or hear a new way to sing something and would keep practicing it on his own. Pahari realized that there was something different about Joshi. He did his work on time and always seemed interested in music. Once Pahari asked Bhimsen to sing at one such rehearsal and Bhimsen was more than happy to oblige. But after hearing him, Pahari was unimpressed. As Bhimsen looked at him eagerly to hear his critique, Pahari Sanyal said simply, "Joshi, if you are thinking of becoming a singer then it would be good to let go of that dream. You sound like a buffalo calf trying to sing. What's more, that calf has a cold!"

Bhimsen was disheartened. But he also knew that if what he had been told was true, then he simply had to get better. He stayed on in the actor's home for a while and then heard about the musical Gharanas in Delhi. But the formidable fees that he was asked to pay ensured that Bhimsen could not stay in Delhi. So he decided to go to Jalandhar, where the Harivallabh Conference was being held. It was at this oldest music conference that the greatest singers from all over the country converged once every year. It was the place to be for all those who found life in music.

Many would have thought the lone but eager boy, travelling on his own across the country, a bit strange. But for Bhimsen, there was no other way. He missed home though and often wondered of a life where he could be close to his family and still pursue music. For now, however, this was his situation. In Jalandhar, Bhimsen was befriended by a wealthy owner of a prosperous cloth mill. The mill owner himself was a talented musician who visited the Harivallabh conference every year. Impressed by Bhimsen's obsession to learn, he offered to buy the young boy his meals every day at a local eatery so he would not have to worry about food. A grateful Bhimsen could resume his search for a Guru in this town with one less worry.

And then he happened to come across the blind singer with the golden voice—Bhakt Mangatram. Bhimsen immediately expressed his wish to learn the Raag Dhrupad from him. Surprised to meet one so young and so passionate, Bhakt Mangatram obliged. He not only taught Bhimsen, but also advised him to absorb music from any of the great performers who were present at the Harivallabh conference. The conference itself was like a festival of music where singers put up many performances.

It was like Bhimsen had discovered an oasis when all he was hoping for was a glass of water. Bhimsen did his homework and found out where a particular singer was performing. After that, he took a Tanpura and obtained the permission to sit behind the singer in his recitals. There for hours, he was given a tutorial on how to raise and lower the pitch, pay attention to intonation and modulate the voice to make it sharp or dense. And the best part of it all was that Bhimsen was getting to learn all of this for free. It was surreal.

A little bit of luck and a whole lot of resilience continued to shape Bhimsen's life. Living in Jalandhar, he learnt a lot from Bhakt Mangatram. He was very grateful to the man who would buy him his meals. And out of respect for this gesture, he never shied away from his practice of music that he kept going at a blistering pace. It was in Jalandhar that Bhimsen also took to physical exercise to pull up his fitness levels. It became a very big reason for him to be able to carry through performances for long hours at a stretch later on in life.

His practice of offering to play the Tanpura for any singer he wished to learn from finally bore fruit. At the Harivallabh conference was Pandit Vinayakrao Patwardhan, a famed singer who had been taught by the Gwalior Gharana. He taught music at the different branches of the Gandharva Mahavidyalaya all over the country and regularly performed at all the music festivals. He was also one of those rare singers whose authored textbooks on music were widely referred. Chance had Bhimsen and Pandit Vinayakrao cross paths at one such performance.

When Vinayakrao heard all the places Bhimsen had gone to in his search of a Guru, he was surprised and impressed by the determination of the young man before him. And then he asked Bhimsen why had he come to Jalandhar to learn the Khayal Gayaki style of singing, when a very big proponent and teacher of the style was present very close to Gadag—Sawai Gandharva, a very famous disciple of Ustad Abdul Karim Khan himself. Sawai Gandharva had a reputation for being a formidable Guru, someone with a quick temper and sharp tongue but uncompromising values in music.

Bhimsen could not believe his ears! It seemed to him that God was trying to tell him something. He had travelled the world searching for something that had been right at home all this while. Life was coming full circle and Bhimsen could not be happier. The path had chosen him from the very beginning and he was finally watching it unfold before him. All he had to do was walk on it without being afraid.

As Bhimsen boarded the train to take him back to Gadag, his heart was light and filled with joy. On reaching home, a tearful reunion with his family followed. So happy were his parents to have him back that his father Gururaj finally accepted his oldest child's decisions and even resolved to take Bhimsen to Pandit Sawai Gandharva and request him to take his son on as a disciple. Bhimsen felt he could not have asked for more from life.

Life could go smoothly for Bhimsen if not for a new problem that was peeking over the horizon. How can a singer protect his voice from the natural progression of life? Bhimsen now faced this highly challenging but very normal problem. The year was 1936, Bhimsen was 14 and his voice was beginning to crack.

While the physical changes of the body are as unavoidable as necessary, for Bhimsen it was a catastrophe of epic proportions. Like all boys his age, his voice was changing because of the rapid growth of the voice box and he did not know what to do about it. He was worried sick if he would be accepted by Pandit Sawai Gandharva at all.

When Pandit Sawai Gandharva was finally told about Bhimsen's problem, he was full of assurance. What Bhimsen did not know then was that many years ago, when Panditji himself was a young boy, he had faced the same problem. Then he had been helped by his own Guru Ustad Khan Sahab by being taught techniques to train the voice to work around this problem. They were techniques of the Kirana Gharana revealed only to the worthy.

Happy to have reached his destination, Bhimsen eagerly awaited his first class with his Guru. Pandit Sawai had agreed to teach Bhimsen at a monthly fee of 25 rupees. But he was taught nothing on the first day. On the second day, he was assigned chores to do around the house and there were still no lessons. By the end of the week, when he had mastered the routine chores he was to do, the formidable Sawai Gandharva gave him more. Chores, that is. Washing clothes, keeping the house clean, fetching water and helping in the kitchen. These were tasks assigned to him and he diligently did them with no protests. He only looked forward to the day Pandit Sawai would finally start his training.

Bhimsen was with his Guru for four years but he was taught only for three. For the first year he was simply made to do chores. Sawai Gandharva was putting to test the young boy's tenacity. It was when he stuck around despite the year of rigorous physical labour that Bhimsen's actual learning began.

Sawai Gandharva was a very dedicated teacher and expected his students to bring nothing but the best into each performance. Bhimsen trained from the break of daylight to dusk. After his singing sessions, he was expected to complete his chores. And if he slipped in any Riyaaz session, the punishment was severe. At one time Sawai Gandharva even hurled a nut-cracker at Bhimsen for under-performing. But this severity showed its worth, when in time he perfected the finer nuances of the Raags Todi, Puriya and Multani which were the specialties of Kirana Gharana.

The four years that Bhimsen spent in the home of Sawai Gandharva was a pleasant time. He always looked back in affection at this phase where he was learning as much as he could and not just lessons in music but also lessons in life. Here were instilled in him the basic qualities of a good artist. One who thoroughly enjoys his performance because only when an artist is true to his art does he touch the hearts of his audience. He had a voice that wasn't high-pitched or sharp as was typical to the Kirana Gharana. Bhimsen's voice was dense. But what he lacked in sound, he made up in melody.

Years passed, Bhimsen was ready for what he had waited all his life. He gave his first live performance in 1941, followed by an album a year later which contained a compilation of devotional songs in Hindi and Kannada. It was a tribute to his mother and grandfather.

The world finally discovered the magic of Bhimsen in 1946 when he sang on his Guru Sawai Gandharva's 60th birthday. Giving it his all, Bhimsen sang like he had never sung before. The audience collectively sighed when he plumbed the depths of sadness in one song; it broke into euphoric applause when he expressed joy in another. This seamless blending of the two faces to life—sorrow and happiness—in the span of one evening, earned him the highest praise and the title of a fitting successor of his celebrated Guru. A critic even asked who this man was, a miracle incarnate.

Over the years, success followed Bhimsen in all of his endeavours. But it was only because of his dedication to his art which involved the exclusion of all else. Awards, appreciation and praise followed him everywhere. But like the great warrior Arjun who had his eye trained only on the eye of the fish, Bhimsen never let go of his one true purpose—his music.

Stories of his dedication are recounted like legends today. And they aren't limited to Bhimsen cycling to a concert because the car broke down; he once had sixteen chillies to cure his cold before a concert so he could avoid its cancellation.

He won the heart of the nation and world with the purity he brought to his music. His love for cars ensured he drove to his performances where he would then perform for eight to nine hours continuously. In fact, so loved was Bhimsen that even the dacoits of Chambal held him in high respects. No sooner did word get around that he was driving through Chambal, he was allowed to pass through undisturbed!

In his fortieth year, Bhimsen performed at a venue in Kolkata one evening. His audience was blown away by his flawless performance of Raags, immaculate breath control and hold over the Kirana Gharana style. The experience was quite unlike anything. Bhimsen had left his own imprint on the Kirana Gharana style of singing and the audience was left asking for more.

After it was over, Bhimsen quietly walked up to the elderly gentleman who had showered much praise on him through the night. Bhimsen then quietly touched the man's feet. The man was shocked. "Sahab, I don't think you recognized me. I had worked in your house as a young boy of ten. You used to call me Joshi," Bhimsen smiled. Pahari

Sanyal was taken aback as recognition slowly dawned on him. Was this the same young boy who sounded like a buffalo calf with cold?

Bhimsen in turn hugged Pahari Sanyal, thanking him. Bhimsen's life was a miracle unfolded and Pahari would have the rest of his life to wonder how this young runaway from Gadag had made it happen…

9

PARDEEP SINGH NAGRA

Stay Winning

As a child, he had loved collecting toy soldiers. With playful courage and conviction, he would enter an imaginary battlefield and entertain an imaginary victory. Perhaps that is how bravery became a firm part of his being, and he had more of it to show wherever he went; despite the threats made to his life, the angry reaction of thousands of people and the pressure from everyone to give up the good fight.

Pardeep Nagra saw himself as a normal person, here on this earth to make a life. He never set out to be the poster boy for courage. He simply did what he thought was the right thing to do. It was an easy enough choice.

For a practicing Sikh in Canada, when he was asked to shave his beard for participating in amateur boxing competitions, it was disconcerting. A beard is one of the basic requisites of his faith. So his refusal to shave his face came not with a surprise. Pardeep instead decided to challenge an archaic rule that was included in the sport not with any rational reasoning save for the aesthetic value it offered. Had he accepted the rule in the chase for a big opportunity, this would have been a different story. But he fought. Not just for himself, but for all those who would come after him.

When he was barely three years old, Pardeep and his family moved to Canada. While born in the land of five rivers, he never got to call Punjab his home. Growing up Pardeep did not wear a turban. Nothing distinguished him from the other South Asian immigrants. More often than not he was mistaken for a Pakistani. Often seemingly innocent activities with his family would flare up into tense situations, and always unprovoked. And even though he was at an age where he couldn't understand it, he could sense that something was not right.

What he did not know then was that Pardeep and his family were experiencing racism firsthand. When they were out together, white people would yell out the words, "Hey Paki" at them. His father, always concerned for the safety of the family, would try the least confrontational approach. He thought that if he kept his cool, the situation would not escalate. But they weren't the only ones. That the entire Sikh community often had to deal with physical and verbal attacks was not unknown to him.

For the young Pardeep, however, this was beyond comprehension. He did not understand why his father, a gentle and hardworking man, would be singled out at a gas station when they went on drives. Random white people would hurl abuses at him, and he would not react to the bullying. Pardeep would often question his father as to why they were always expected to keep quiet while strangers would walk away after insulting them. He often felt that even when they weren't responding to the insults, the abusers knew that Pardeep and his family were scared of them. His father would then explain to him why indulging the bullies with a reaction

was always a bad idea. One bad word uttered in retaliation could turn a bad situation into a crime scene.

Such were the ways to make it in this foreign land. In order to blend in, people would often be forced to shed their signs of identity, the remnants of their old country. So when Pardeep grew his hair, his tied up bun stood out as a marker of his identity, different from others, making him an easy target. But instead of cutting off his hair, he consciously chose to live by the tenets of his faith in his teen years. He chose to work on other ways that could help him blend in, instead.

At his own level, Pardeep thought that if he did well academically, people would be more accepting of him. He studied hard and did well in school. But it was at sports that he soon discovered he was a natural. He was ready for anything. Whether running, soccer, ball hockey, table tennis or even boxing, there was nothing that Pardeep wouldn't want to play. And what's more, he simply enjoyed competing with other people in sports and winning.

The more he was involved in sports, Pardeep realized, the more his fellow students and seniors at school noticed him. Was it respect? Pardeep soon realized being good at sports made it hard for people to sideline him. And since competition in sports was a great equalizer, the insults were slowly getting replaced with admiration. He did not take this for granted and pushed himself to the limit no matter what he played. When he won, which was often, it was because of his efforts and the discipline in training. His dedication to sports stood Pardeep in good stead. His name began to get included among the best athletes at school. He was finally beginning to feel the one thing he wanted the most from this place he called his home—acceptance.

Between academics and sports, Pardeep barely had time for anything else. The toy soldiers of childhood had left their impact, maybe that's why he applied to enroll with the Police force, and got through. His selection was a source of immense pride to his parents. They were glad that their son was now going to make sure that no one had to experience the darker side of making life in a new country.

One day, during a regular Soccer match, Pardeep injured his shoulder. Soon, what had seemed like a minor injury turned out to be a major one. The shoulder had to be operated upon. But with his enrollment with the Peel Regional Police, Pardeep could not take time off. There was no way he could skip training. If he took time off now, he would have to re-apply for the services and go through the whole selection process again. He decided to go ahead with the training and focus on healing his shoulder after the training was finished.

While training, Pardeep had to give a lot of thought to how he would take care of his injury. He realized that gymnasts and even boxers had very strong upper bodies. In order to work on his shoulder, he would have to pick one. And since he was quite old to take up gymnastics, serendipity left him with boxing as his only option.

The more he studied the science of boxing and all that it entailed, the more fascinated he became. Every aspect of the sport like training the body, the mind, focusing on building endurance got him deeply interested. After reading up all he could about boxing, Pardeep joined a boxing gymnasium called Jamestown and Champion boxing gym with Coach Dewith Frazer. Since the exercises involved building muscles in the shoulders and arms, Pardeep dived straight in. All the hard work he channeled into boxing made him realise that he enjoyed it. And he had not even entered the boxing ring as yet.

One day, as Pardeep was busy practicing his jabs, a fellow boxer asked him if he ever planned to get into the ring. Pardeep instinctively said he would like that. What he was told next stunned him. He was told that should he ever want to compete, he would have to shave his beard first if he wanted to fight in the ring.

That was the first time he had come across this bizarre rule. Pardeep went to ask his Coach Frazer if it was indeed mandatory for all boxers to shave their beards. The Coach was not sure and offered to look up the rule. When he did, he realized that it was in fact stipulated by law that boxers in competitive boxing could not have beards. They were allowed to have neatly trimmed moustaches and sideburns. Since his beard was an article of faith, he held a naïve hope that he could be an exception to the rule and that the Canadian Amateur Boxing Association (CABA) would surely consider his case.

In Canada, all boxers who compete in boxing competitions as amateurs have to follow the rules of the CABA. Not convinced, he began digging for the reasons of this rule. He was told that the rule was made keeping in mind the health and safety of the competitors. *Somehow, long beards posed a health hazard in the ring?* He was confused. So the next thing he did was ask doctors how beards could be a health or safety challenge. He got many explanations but none that seemed reasonable enough.

In an attempt to understand what he was up against, Pardeep now decided to look up the origins of the rule. After all, this rule could possibly be the biggest hurdle in his chance to compete. He discovered that the rule had British origins and was even more surprised that it applied to Policemen and several other professions.

It was clear now to Pardeep that to enter the boxing ring he would first have to take up a different fight outside it. After a lot of thought, he challenged the Association with the help of a lawyer on the rule that prohibited competitors from keeping beards.

With respect to the same, a proposal was put before the Canadian Amateur Boxing Association during its Annual General Meeting. It was sent by Pardeep and his lawyer and asked for the CABA to allow Pardeep to compete in the amateur boxing despite his beard, which was kept for religious reasons only. The CABA decided to take a vote and the proposal was ruled out with nine people against it and six in favour.

Most people would have considered this a big blow and re-thought their stand. But for Pardeep, this was not a battle of egos. It was simply his assertion of his beliefs. And so, he chose to look at the bright side. If six people did believe he was in the right, there was scope to convince more. Now, on the advice of his lawyer, Pardeep filed a complaint with the human rights body. He expressed to the Ontario Human Rights that his right to follow his faith was being violated due to the rules made by Boxing Ontario.

In a move that left him and everyone else surprised, Ontario Human Rights sided with Pardeep and got Boxing Ontario to alter the rules. Pardeep was now allowed to compete in the boxing matches within Ontario as an exception. Thrilled with the breakthrough, Pardeep began to train for the Ontario Provincial Novice Championships with renewed zeal. He had Coach Frazer by his side all the while. And after having won one fight, Pardeep won the championship too.

A hard worker with an eye for detail, Pardeep had always trained enthusiastically. Winner of the Ontario Novice Provincial Championships, he was now qualified to represent his province Ontario in the National level championships that were to be held soon. If he won the national competition, he would be eligible to represent the country of Canada in the Sydney Olympics to be held the following year in 2000. This was a source of immense inspiration that kept him going. Until the day he received a notice that stated that Pardeep was not allowed to compete in the Canadian National Championships. He was taken aback. Having come so far, he was not anticipating such a move from a body of national stature. He only had one way to go. Pardeep went back to the court. This time the court stood in his favour too and directed the CABA to allow Pardeep to compete in the National Championships.

But before he could relish this big win, in an unexpected move, CABA cancelled the weight class, the measurement weight range, in which Pardeep was to compete. This was a shocker and proved to be the toughest part of Pardeep's battle. He was immediately sidelined. His life was threatened while jealous rival boxers rejoiced. Being at the receiving end of extremely racist threats became common for him. Considering the sensitivity and stress of the situation, Pardeep's parents too began to feel that it was too heavy a price to pay for keeping a beard. He was encouraged by his family to finally make a choice; it was either boxing or his beard.

But for Pardeep, there was no way he would give up what he loved just because of some old rules that stood irrelevant in today's age. Despite the threats he received, he went back to the court to get a final decision as far as the rules at CABA were concerned.

With his lawyer, he began to strengthen his case. It so happened that before he could present his case to the Canadian Amateur Boxing Association, Pardeep met one of their representatives. He asked the man why they were so unwilling to change the rule. To his surprise, CABA, which until then had been in favour of the rule on health and safety grounds, now changed its position.

The representative of CABA told Pardeep that they could not allow beards since a beard would give the player an unfair advantage. Pardeep was a reasonable man. His humour shone through as he reasoned that if beards can cushion the blows of an opponent, then every player in boxing must be encouraged to grow beards, including female boxers! He asked the CABA representative shouldn't they be making beards mandatory instead, since their sole job is to make rules that make sports safer.

No sooner had the representative spoken to Pardeep, CABA again changed its position for opposing beards due to reasons of health and safety. Pardeep fought on, stating that if beards were such a hazard in sports, why was it allowed in other Mixed Martial Art and Combat sports. While inside the court, Pardeep fought bravely, the public outside subjected him and his family to rather extreme racist abuse. But with the end goal firmly in his mind, Pardeep kept telling himself that the fight may be hard right now, but it will pave an easier path for all those who will come after him.

They say when one fights the good fight, they start out lonely, but eventually support follows. Soon, Trivial Pursuit, a very popular board game based on general knowledge and pop culture questions, included a question on Pardeep in one of its editions. Other major publications featured Pardeep, some alongside Prime Ministers and other noted personalities.

The climax to his struggle in the court involved a victory. Boxing in Canada would now allow players to keep their beards. The greatest happiness for him was when he won the court case and CABA was forced to amend its rules. It was not just a win for Pardeep, but a message from the people of Canada that as long as no one was getting hurt, he had the full freedom to practice his faith. For Pardeep this was a fight far different and necessary than the one he could now have in the ring. It too had tested his grit and determination and the mettle of his loved ones and himself. Through it all, he had fought on, and like the imaginary soldiers of his childhood fantasies, emerged victorious.

10

SUBHAS CHANDRA BOSE

Faith and Freedom

The year was 1919. An interview was under process for a candidate not so ordinary. To appear for it was a privilege granted only to a few British citizens. And Indians who qualified for it were so rare they might as well have been unicorns!

Only those candidates who had cleared the written exam were allowed to appear for this interview that Subhas Chandra Bose was sitting for.

The interview was to shortlist officers who would serve in India, then a very rich colony of the British. The officers were selected through the Indian Civil Services Exams which comprised of a written exam and an interview. The exam, considered one of the toughest in the world at that time, was cleared by Subhas, who stood fourth in merit and also managed to impress his detractors in the process.

Selection in the Indian Civil Service meant the twenty-three-year old Subhas was all set to live a life of opulence and luxury. But it was not money or power that he dreamt of. All that mattered to him was the well-being of his parents. And the job would have secured him that.

Why then did the thought of accepting it fill him with revulsion? For Subhas it was a deal with the devil. Working for the British meant he would be forced to turn a blind eye to their actions and also aid them in exploiting his own country. How could he serve them knowing what they were doing to his own people?

Always the reason for his parent's anxiety, Subhas had moved to England to assure them he wouldn't cause any trouble. All that was expected of him was that he gives up his wayward ways of insisting that the British leave India. His father Jankinath himself was a successful lawyer on the side of the British. He often wondered why his son couldn't follow suit. And now Subhas had in his hand the chance to finally do what would make his father happy and settle down to a life of comfort and safety. But in his heart, he wanted to resign from the post and to do it with the blessings of his parents.

Troubled, Subhas picked up the pen. He would have to bare his heart to them. "Mother and Father…" he began writing his letter. He told them how this work would bring him tremendous unhappiness and that for a man like him, the glories of the world held no attraction. He wanted to serve his country and he would be unable to do so were he chained to the civil service. And then he waited for an answer back…

"There were many reasons. But the primary one was the erosion of loyalty to the British crown amongst the Indian Army and Navy soldiers because of the military activities of Netaji."

These were the words of Clement Attlee, who was the Prime Minister of Britain at the time when India became independent in 1947. When Attlee came to India on a visit in 1956 as a guest of the Governor of West Bengal, Shri P. R. Chakraborthy, he was asked why Britain left India at a time when it was running the strongest empire on earth. Their World War II victory had ensured that Britain could have ruled India for another hundred years if they so wished.

For the world, India gained independence from British rule on 15th August 1947. But for Indians, in a way, independence had arrived on 14th April 1944. It was the day that the Azad Hind Fauj or the Indian National Army made its way through Japanese controlled Burma, trekked the Naga Hills and silently entered Manipur. Here, the brave soldiers fought and defeated the British. The act was a wake-up call for the British that India was capable of making silent, victorious moves. It was in this small state on the 14th of April that the tricolour was unfurled for the first time on Indian soil. And it was from this day on that the hearts of the entire nation were moved in unison towards a single cause of complete Independence.

The man behind this wave of nationalism was Subhas Chandra Bose. For the people he was Netaji, a name given to him in love and reverence.

Netaji was known for his genius, his vision, his mind. An excellent strategist and diplomat par excellence, he approached Hitler to convince him that the cause for Indian independence was so justified that India deserved to be helped in setting up an army to fight. So famed was he as an effective arbitrator that even Muhammad Ali Jinnah—the man who desired the partition of British India into India and Pakistan—had openly said that if Netaji had remained in India, there would have been no partition. Even Mahatma Gandhi declared during partition that had Netaji been alive, there would have been no Pakistan.

Netaji was born into privilege but chose a life of hardships, solely to be able to see his fellow Indians live with dignity in their own country. He chose the nation over self at every chance that arrived.

Born in Cuttack, on the 23rd of January 1897, he was the ninth child of Prabhavati, a home-maker and Jankinath, a lawyer and government pleader. Jankinath had done very well rooting himself firmly on the side of the British, and in one of God's ironic ploys, a man so loyal to the colonizers of his land became father to a son who would forever be loyal to his own people.

Subhas was a shy youngster. An introvert, he preferred to observe from the side rather than be the centre of attention. Having seen his older siblings go to school made him look forward to it, so the five-year-old Subhas was excited to see the sight of the tonga that would take him to school. In his joy, he ran towards it, tripped and fell, injuring his foot. The first day of school did not happen for him on this account, and it was then that he was brought to tears. Following a small hiccup in the beginning, soon Subhas would go on to extract all that he could from his classes. He learnt a lot about the British, their history, culture, science as well as their customs and way of life. But dissatisfaction followed him around. He often wondered why there was no subject on Hindi, Sanskrit or Indian History. When he questioned this practice, he was often told to not worry himself with such trivialities and to concentrate on his studies instead. While he distinguished himself in sports as well as academics, these questions continued to bother him.

"Why do we have so much, Ma? And why is it that everywhere I look, I see everyone suffering and living in so much poverty?" Subhas would often pose these questions to his gentle mother. While Prabhavati would not be able to allay all his doubts, it was she who instilled in his heart the desire to help others. She would often tell him that helping others was the nourishment of your own soul.

Subhas still continued searching for answers which led him to read the works of the mystic Ramakrishna Paramhansa and his disciple, Hindu monk and philosopher, Swami Vivekananda at the tender age of twelve. He soon began to consider them his idols. But his parents were in for a shock when Subhas began to talk about wanting to live like them, as a Yogi and help the poorest of the poor. The teachings of Vivekananda did not just help Subhas shape his life, they even helped him conquer his fears. Always plagued by bad dreams and a crippling fear of the dark, Subhas had finally found a way out of their grip.

Soon Subhas went to the famed Presidency college for higher studies. If life in Cuttack had somewhat acquainted Subhas with reality, here in Calcutta, Subhas saw its darker side. Discrimination against Indians was rampant and it was not unusual for a student to be thrashed by a teacher for no real reason. At this time, the nation was wrecked by constant famines and the British were not of much help. There were unclothed, poor, starving, homeless people everywhere. Meanwhile discrimination and oppression against Indians was increasing by the day.

Being a good student, Subhas did not waver from excellence in academics. But he gravitated towards the students who thought like him, people who read and followed the teachings of Vivekananda and Paramhansa. He had begun to spend far more time with the revolutionaries who wanted to oust the British from India forever. Subhas could often be found on the streets of the city begging for food that they could give to the needy. But no matter how much he did, it never seemed enough.

He began to lose interest in studies and wanted to work for the poor instead. He avoided going home for the holidays since his parents urged him to give up what he was doing. Instead, he and his group of friends would go to villages. Once when they were about to enter one such village, the people there took one look at them and began to shout. Subhas was baffled, until eventually the villagers realized their mistake and apologized. Embarrassed and weeping, they admitted they thought they were tax collectors. The villagers had nothing to feed even themselves with, but the cruel tax collectors showed no mercy, extracting their pound of flesh anyhow.

It was when the student council at the Presidency College made Subhas the President that the teachers got their first taste of his sense of justice. There was a teacher called Mr E. F. Oaten who had the reputation for having a rough temper and thrashing Indian students and making anti-India remarks. Subhas once lost his patience after hearing about another case of Oaten beating up an Indian student, and went calmly to the principal, Mr Henry Rosher James, demanding Oaten apologises or the students would go on a mass strike. While the principal assured him that he would look into the matter, no action was taken. Oaten continued to walk about brashly, hurling even more abuses on the students. Subhas soon asked the students to stop attending college and for the first time in the history of the Presidency College, a mass strike was organized.

With the matter drawing the attention of the nation, the college's reputation was suffering an immense loss. To put the fire out, Subhas was promised that Professor Oaten would apologise to the concerned student and he did so too. The strike was called off. But things took a turn for the worse when Oaten hit yet another student with double the vengeance this time.

When this reached the ears of Subhas, he knew precisely what had to be done next. A few days later Professor Oaten was beaten by several Indian students as payback for all that he had done. He was left to writhe in pain as the students made their way back to the hostel.

The next day, the Principal of the college called Subhas and demanded an explanation for the assault on the professor. Subhas declined to say anything only for the principal to make several allegations against him and berate him for attacking the professor behind his back. Confident in what he had done, Subhas was quick to tell the principal that only cowards hit from the back. He had stood face to face with the professor. The principal was stunned. Not only had he boldly admitted to attacking the professor but also showed no remorse for it.

Professor Oaten never did muster the courage to lash out at anyone after this.

However, at the moment, the principal had had enough. Subhas was expelled from the college with immediate effect. When the news was out, all the students came out in open support of Subhas. He openly complained about the discrimination that was meted out to the Indian students, how often punishment was given to students without reason, and how they were expected to swallow insults in their own country for being Indian. He justified the assault on the grounds that Oaten, despite being given several chances, had never reformed his actions.

Normally, Indians toed the line that was expected of them. They were powerless to challenge the social order. And here was a young man, unbothered by the harsh consequences of speaking the truth. To no one's surprise then, Subhas was expelled from the college. His family was shocked. While they were sure that his future was ruined forever, he was sure he would continue fighting for what was right. In an attempt to get him back on the right path, he was enrolled in the Scottish College in Cuttack.

While his parents hoped and prayed that their ninth offspring begins to live the life that was expected of him, Subhas's beliefs about the oppression of his people and how there was a need to take action against it were solidifying into a changed worldview. Prabhavati Devi was desperate to have her son back into the family fold, but he felt like a different man now. He would tell her that she had thirteen children to look after her; one was needed to look after Mother Hind too. Subhas knew the effect his words would have on his parents and so he tried his best to make them happy. He performed very well in academics, going on to complete his master's in philosophy by 1918.

But his mind was made up. His life was dedicated for the people. India was ravaged by the plague, cholera and malaria due to rampant famine. More than two lakh people died during this time. Subhas would go around arranging free medicine for the affected people. Not just that, many unclaimed bodies were cremated respectfully with Subhas taking the responsibility to perform their last rites.

Jankinath couldn't watch his son take on the burdens of the world. To ease his father's mind, Subhas's older brother convinced Subhas to go to London and prepare for the Indian Civil Service Exams. He reasoned with Subhas that if he cleared the exam, he could work on laws in favour of the Indians.

In the light of his parent's anxiety and his brother's proposition, Subhas agreed with the plan Sarat had proposed and decided to leave for the Fitzwilliam College in Cambridge, London in 1919. The fact the ICS exam was considered one of the toughest in the world did not worry him. With thoughts of his motherland in his heart, Subhas set sail for a country that signified the word 'oppressor' for him all his life so far.

Cambridge was a revelation to Subhas. While he missed being home, he was surprised to see that the Indians here were not relegated to the background or subjected to constant physical and verbal abuse. Instead, unexpectedly, they were treated like normal people. The atmosphere at the college was favourable to the growth of an individual and so indirectly, the whole nation. Subhas realized that India would forever be a slave if each and every man, woman and child was not allowed to think freely.

But not one to lose sight of his purpose, Subhas concentrated solely on cracking the ICS exam. He was a bright scholar and put in the work to clear the exam and that is why when the results were declared, he was surprised to see that his name was not on the list. Disappointed that he had let his parents down, he was sitting by himself when a friend came rushing to him to congratulate. Subhas was confused. On hearing his words, his friend began to laugh and told him that his name was not on the list of students who had cleared the exam because his name was on the list of toppers. Subhas had not only cleared the exam but he stood fourth amongst all candidates that had appeared! Now all he had to do was clear the interview and he was set for life.

After impressing his interviewer and scoring a perfect hundred, Subhas was selected for one of the most exclusive jobs in the strongest empire in the world at that time.

Life had given Subhas a golden opportunity. And now that he was so close to getting all that his parents had wanted for him, he was unsure. How could a son watch the destruction of his motherland? But how could a son disappoint his parents? Everything that happened next depended on the letter he was to receive back.

Finally, an answer arrived. It was from his mother. All the weeks that Subhas had spent worrying were immediately forgotten with the letter. She wrote to him that he should go ahead and do what his heart desired. She knew that this decision would greatly anger his father but she also knew that in his heart Subhas had already dedicated himself to the country. And she could not be the one to stop him.

Her words were the light Subhas had been looking for in the dark. Without the slightest hesitation, he sent in his resignation.

On the ship back to Bombay, Subhas had plenty of time to think about what his next step would be. Right now India was shackled by slavery, poverty and disease. The wealth and resources she was famous for were depleting at the hands of her conquerors. Indians had been suppressed for so long that they had forgotten of the time when they were free. But all was not lost yet. There were many like him who dreamt of breathing in a free India and they were willing to fight for it. Like the vast and endless ocean ahead of him, full of hope, Subhas could sense endless opportunities that awaited a free India. The ship soon docked in Bombay on a bright and humid morning in June.

For his efforts, he was beaten, thrashed and jailed more than a dozen times. That his and his family's name was dragged into the mud was another price he paid for standing up to the British. In his thirties, Subhas was released from jail and went on to become the Mayor of Kolkata. At this time, he had power, influence and money and was hobnobbing with powerful leaders. But as the editor of a newspaper, his revolutionary views brought him into direct conflict with the British. He was arrested again and sent abroad to Mandalay in prison. But even prison could not make him give up his beliefs. Released in his forties, he was still widely revered by the public and was made the president of the Indian National Congress.

With the love and support of a nation behind him and the British distracted with preparations for World War II, all Subhas had to do was wait and not denounce Gandhiji's way of attaining independence as ineffective. But to turn the other cheek was not the way Subhas envisioned the attainment of Swaraj. He could not get himself to agree with Gandhiji on things he fundamentally thought wrong. And so, he resigned from the Congress Working Committee, despite standing for election against a candidate supported by Gandhiji.

In the cold winter of January 1941, Subhas was under house arrest in his house at Elgin Road in Kolkata. This was after his release from prison in December 1940. Finally, it seemed Subhas would settle down to a quiet life. Unbothered by the armed guards outside his door, he was free to follow a life of reading and writing. But for him, this life felt hollow. It was time to make a move. Disguising himself as a Pakhtun from Afghanistan, Subhas orchestrated an escape from the British that made its way well into history as one of the finest feats he ever achieved.

He then hitch-hiked a ride on a submarine to Sumatra and sealed his friendship with the Japanese Prime Minister Hideki. When he asked Tojo how outsiders were ruling Asia when it did not belong to them, he had found a friend and ally for life. With Tojo's support, Subhas raised the Azad Hind Fauj or Indian National Army, entered India through Myanmar and fought the British on Indian soil. He didn't just defeat their army; he delivered a mortal blow to the psyche of invincibility that the British had developed. That's how the INA raised the Indian National Flag in Manipur for the first time on 14th April 1944.

But all of this was on the distant horizon of his future. Right now, as he stepped back on the Indian land, he was hopeful. They could throw the British out of the country if they all joined hands. And that day would surely come; Subhas believed in it till his very last breath.

11

CHEWANG NORPHEL

The Ice Man

"There is no God!" shouted Lhamo looking up at the heavens, his voice heart-broken and pained. Colourful paper flags strung on a monastery nearby fluttered in the wind as an answer. There seemed no respite from this life which was full of hardships, loss and hard work.

There was no-one to hear him, as he stood at the base of the mountain where his land was, in the village of Phuktse. Tears sprung in his eyes when he looked at the saplings of wheat he had sown. He had spent days and weeks ploughing, levelling and manuring this land. He had taken a day long trip to the city of Leh to select the best quality of wheat seeds so that he would have a good quality crop. It was an expense he could do without but everything was worth a healthy crop. And not just the seeds, but the manure and fertilizers he chose were of good quality. After all, the yield by this crop was to sustain him and his family for a long time. No effort was too big a cost.

Lhamo came from a long line of farmers. He lived in the small village of Phuktse in Ladakh. Despite all his efforts, Lhamo had the wisdom to remind himself that even if he got a fifty percent yield, he would be a lucky man. Maybe this year, the God of rain and water would be merciful.

Hope was all he had.

But even hope, it seemed, had deserted Lhamo and his village. The rains had deserted them this year. And their last recourse, that made agriculture possible in the cold desert of Ladakh, the natural glaciers and snow had greatly reduced too.

Helplessly, Lhamo watched his crop die. The loan he had taken to sow it would loom over his head for a long time. He had no idea how he would pay it back. Taught by his mother since childhood that God protects the honest and the hard working, he had lived a simple life, worked for every grain he fed his family and had never wronged anyone. And yet here he was, a failure of his labour staring him in the face. He wondered for a moment if his mother had lied to him. Because if there was a God, how could he be this unfair and let all his efforts go in vain? How could he watch Lhamo, his parents, his wife and children starve?

No. A God who could do this was no God at all. Lhamo wiped his tears and without another glance at his dying crop, walked away.

In this misery, he was not alone. In a land where agriculture was a way of life for 80% of the total population, there were thousands like Lhamo who shared his fate. A lot of them swallowed the bitter pill of disappointment and waited for the next year to bring them water for their crop of wheat or barley. A small number from among them chose death as the way out of this loop.

Chewang felt uneasy as he sipped on his yak butter tea while reading his newspaper on that cold morning, early in

June. He had just read about yet another suicide by a helpless middle-aged farmer because the rains had failed them. News like this had become more common of late. The year was 1987 and Chewang Norphel, a fifty-two-year-old retired civil engineer, was reading his morning paper while his wife busied herself in readying breakfast.

Born in 1935 into a family of farmers, Chewang was very deeply attached to the land. He was an interesting child, harboring love for his home and a fascination for the world. A curious child, he was interested in all things, especially numbers. When out pasturing the goats, he'd let them off to graze meanwhile flipping out a small, worn notebook, scribbling away furiously, awed by the wonder that he thought was maths. He was deeply inspired by his father's brother, Sonam Norbu, who was sent to London for higher studies and was the first person in Ladakh to become an engineer by profession. On coming back, he worked on building Ladakh's first airport, a web of roads connecting various towns and cities in Ladakh and other infrastructure. Chewang too wanted a life where his work could prove useful to generations of people.

Growing up, Chewang's life was a simple one. He spent his time playing and squabbling away with his brother and sister, helping in chores and doing his studies. But on completing his primary education, while he expected to go to secondary school, Chewang was asked to get himself ordained as a monk and follow the spiritual path of life. He knew the reason for this was lack of money.

For the little ten-year-old, a life spent in pursuing God by reading and studying about Him, was not ideal. So a dark, cold night found Chewang running away from home without a warning or a plan. His destination lay more than four hundred kilometres away; past steep mountain passes and dangerous terrains. With no plan in place, Chewang reached Srinagar tired and hungry but determined as ever and made his way to the only place he wanted to be at—a school.

Once there, he realized that he would not be allowed to sit through classes in return for nothing. Young and desperate, he approached the teachers and proposed to let him cook and clean for them. All he wanted in return was a place to stay and complete his education. The universe was willing to help the little boy, for his efforts did not go to waste and he was soon sitting for secondary school classes.

A sharp mind and hard work ensured that Chewang aced his studies. He went on to earn a degree in Science from Amar College in Srinagar followed by a Diploma in Civil Engineering from Lucknow. He was an engineer now; the dream nurtured in childhood had been realized, and he had done it all on his own. As a newly independent country, India needed sharp minds that were willing to set her on the path of progress. This dawn of the free country was Chewang's oyster. He could go wherever he wanted to and earn well. But there was only one place Chewang set out for. And that was home.

As someone who wanted to make a difference, Chewang lost no time in getting to work. Upon the completion of his Diploma, he went back to Leh and was selected for the job of a Rural Civil Engineer. Coming from an agrarian family, he had seen first-hand, all the problems that farmers faced. From lack of equipment and tools to availability of timely information on the weather and water shortages, Chewang was aware of it all. He finally had the means to improve the lives of his people just like his uncle had done and undertook many projects of building infrastructure. Among the 120 villages in Ladakh, barely was a village left where Chewang had not built a hut, a bridge or a road.

Sandwiched between the Himalayan and the Karakoram Range of mountains, Ladakh is one of the highest inhabited places on earth. Since it lies in the rain shadow area of the Himalayas, by the time the clouds arrive here, they have already lost their moisture. As a result, the rainfall here is scarce making it the only place where one can get dehydrated and frost bitten at the same time!

For Chewang, the matter of water shortage was nothing new. All the inhabitants of Ladakh constantly encountered it. The difference was, now he had the power to do something about it, and he began with helping in the construction of Zings, artificially constructed tanks used to store and harvest water from melted water of the glaciers.

It seemed things would not be so bad after all. With the construction of Zings and the melted water from glaciers, the farmers would be able to manage even if the rains did not arrive on time. Chewang felt certain things would get better.

Traditionally, large amounts of snowfall every year would ensure glaciers would be replenished to provide water for agriculture and sustenance. But an unseen enemy was creeping into Ladakh. And the people were not ready to face it…

A direct result of human activity, climate change meant a permanent shift in the normal temperatures of the earth. With the earth warming up, the rise of even a degree in the temperature meant utter chaos in the already fragile water cycle of Ladakh. As a result, the snowfall in Ladakh was directly hit by the climate change of the last few decades. The average snowfall in Ladakh began to reduce, melting before the spring season. This meant that farmers began to get lesser water during sowing season which is March and April. At the same time, the glaciers that provided much needed irrigation for the crop as it grew, had begun to shrink higher up on the mountain. By the time they melted, it was too late to be of use for the crops.

Another downside of shrinking glaciers meant the grass that was the pasture for goats and sheep, retreated even higher up the mountains. Since farmers could not accompany their cattle so high up, they were left to survive on their own while grazing. Attacks by leopards became a constant threat. As a result, farmers who had lived on the land were forced to leave, migrating to the city to pursue other professions.

Chewang is a true Buddhist whose firm faith demanded that the way to live was to help others. And as someone who had made it his job to look after the well-being of his people, the problem of water shortage was one that everyone hoped he would tackle. One solution, he was told by his superiors, was to build concrete dams. They would hold enough water for the people as well as for irrigation. The more Chewang delved into the process of building dams, the more convinced he was that it was not just an expensive and time-consuming process, but it also caused irreparable damage to the environment and to the people who would be displaced from the land of their ancestors to make way for its construction.

Another winter morning and another newspaper brought the same news of yet another farmer's suicide, making

Chewang feel a familiar restlessness come over him. They would just have to find a different solution.

To get a hold of himself, he stepped outside into his backyard, his favourite place to unwind. He practiced growing vegetables here, on a small scale. He often experimented with different vegetables to see if they would thrive in the cold climes of Ladakh.

But today he was not in the mood to do anything. He ran his eyes at the landscape, spotting the village water faucet under a poplar tree at a distance. The faucet brought water to Chewang's backyard all through the year. It was never turned off. Rather, it could not be turned off since in winter the water in the turned off faucet would freeze causing the pipe to burst. What Chewang noticed was that today, while the water from the faucet ran to join the stream, under the shade of the tree, it froze to form pools. These ice pools had grown in size with each passing day. In stark contrast, the water in the river a few yards ahead, ran without freezing.

Come spring, the water in the pools slowly melted and disappeared. Could there not be a way to create shallow pools of ice where water could be stored in winter, to melt during spring and provide water for crops? Besides, all the natural glaciers were situated at a height of 5000 feet above sea level. They melted only in June and even then, since they were situated about 20 to 25 kilometres away from most villages, to divert their water to the fields in the village was an expensive proposition.

Chewang wondered what if there were glaciers at lower altitudes which could melt sooner due to changing temperatures. They could easily provide timely water to crops during sowing season. Besides, man had learned to make use of solar and thermal energy. In Ladakh they had cold energy. The cold on this land could freeze anything. It was only reasonable that what they had in plenty must be put to good use. The more Chewang thought, the less impossible the idea seemed.

So lost was he in this thought, that he did not even hear when he was called in for lunch by his wife. Upon being disturbed from his reverie, he looked at her and said, "All you have to do is reduce the velocity of water. And it freezes." His wife simply nodded her head without comment. She then watched Chewang go straight to his study. All these years of watching him work told her another big idea had struck her husband.

Closing himself in his study, Chewang excitedly began to draw some basic design structures. In winters the severe cold made it impossible to grow crops, making the water in streams go to waste. If they could conserve this water in the form of ice, this water could be used in for the irrigation season. As far as the freezing of the water was concerned, Chewang already had an answer in mind. He drew a series of diagrams depicting the water in the streams being slowed by a series of walls. The slow movement of the water would freeze it just like a glacier.

The streams that were wide and located on gentle slopes would directly form frozen sheets of ice and snow. For the narrower streams located on steep slopes, he had another idea. They would first be diverted to gentler slopes through several water channels before they were allowed to freeze. If the glacier was made close to the village and in the shadow area of the mountain, the ice would melt just in time for sowing season ensuring adequate water for the farmers.

All they had to do was make these artificial glaciers at different levels, situating them between the natural glaciers and the village. That way the lower glaciers would provide much needed water for crops, while the higher glaciers would serve as water reservoirs.

Going over the idea again and again, Chewang felt confident they had finally made a breakthrough in solving the water crisis. In a land where fresh water is more precious than oil especially after summer, he had managed to use a mix of common sense and science to solve a long-standing problem.

Armed with sketches and adequate research, Chewang began to show his idea to government officials. But like they say, no good deed goes unpunished. He asked for funds so that he could begin to implement the idea as soon as possible. To his surprise, not only was he denied the funds, he was also called *pagal* for proposing such an idea. Some villagers, who heard what Chewang was proposing, joined the army of people who thought that Chewang had lost his mind for making such a silly proposition. That a glacier, formations they had witnessed for time immemorial, could artificially be made to treat a specific issue confounded most.

Undefeated, Chewang continued to pitch his idea to any official who was willing to listen. A lot of them heard him out of respect but help was far from coming. In the meantime, the constant news of farmers being pushed to the extent of killing themselves all because of the lack of water made Chewang desperate. All his life he had been asked to look for a solution. Now when he had found it, that he was called mad did not bother him. What bothered him was that in not giving his idea a chance, they had put at stake the lives of many other farmers who could be saved.

Still Chewang moved ahead. He left no stone unturned in getting officials to help. But with no funds to aid him, he finally decided to try and convince the villagers. They would have to make the artificial glacier themselves to see how it could help them.

And so, it was that one morning, among the villagers of Phuktse stood Chewang, eager to tell them how they could have water for their crop when they needed it the most. He explained to them how they could artificially make the glaciers they had been seeing since their birth. They would make them six to seven thousand feet below the natural glaciers. These artificial glaciers would melt during sowing season, providing the much-needed irrigation sources the farmers needed. He also explained to them how these glaciers would replenish ground water. Once the ground water level in the earth went up, Chewang promised them that the numerous springs that had been drying up, would be regenerated making Ladakh the place of their childhood once more.

The villagers heard him out. Chewang was honest enough to tell them that while they did not have any backing or funds, they would have to undertake this mission on their own. No sooner had the men heard that, they began to laugh. "Do you really think that we will give up farming and come and work on this new-found idea of yours? And that too for no money?" they questioned.

Chewang watched as the laughter around him grew. They began to find flaws in his plan, poking fun at him. "You city folk come up with such outrageous ideas to entertain yourselves. It is we peasant folk who pay the price. What will we get out of wasting our time and breaking our backs on this idea of yours?" asked one of them. "We are poor people sir, we can't take off from our work just like that," was the general refrain.

But Chewang refused to back down. He said, "I know I don't have anything to give you in return. But don't you see? This glacier will set you free from your dependence on the rain. If you will give up a few days of work to build this, you will end up making a brighter future for your own children who will never have to worry about their crops failing due to lack of water."

While the rest of the villagers of Phuktse were busy calling Chewang's proposal worthless, Lhamo heard the commotion and followed. "Who is he and what does he want?" he asked his neighbour who had been listening to Chewang all this while. "He is *pagal*, a mad man. He is proposing we build a glacier on our own to help water our crops. He says we will never have to worry about the rains coming on time if we help him make this artificial glacier on our own."

Chewang came back from Phuktse empty handed since no villager was willing to put their money or time into his idea. But he refused to give up. He knew this project could work. He just needed one person to believe in him.

The next day, the villagers were surprised to see Chewang before them again. This time, instead of making pleas, he was working, quietly and patiently. He lifted and placed brick-sized stones. The villagers laughed at this mad man who was back again, stubborn that he was. But by afternoon, a few villagers joined in laying and placing the stones. And by the evening, what looked like a trickle, turned into a flood of workers ready to make real, the idea Chewang was so committed to…

So successful was the artificial glacier of Phuktse that Chewang went on to make 17 such glaciers all across Ladakh. Chewang and the villagers were able to solve one of the most recurring problems faced by the beautiful valley of Ladakh. Slowly this lone ranger received support not just from the villagers but the state-run government programs, the Indian Army as well as various non-government organisations. Whether it proved really useful was answered next year, when farmers like Lhamo stood smiling before their healthy crops.

Yes, Chewang had dreamed the impossible. And what was more; he had made it come true. This cold desert was now undergoing a change for the better. There was more water, the number of trees had increased dramatically because of which the water levels had risen greatly. Things were starting to look good finally.

Lhamo too had exactly these thoughts that morning when he looked up to the sky, happier than he had ever been. Maybe God was real. A miracle like the work of Chewang could not have happened otherwise.

12

SANJIT ROY

Lighting a Revolution

"No. I won't allow it!" On hearing her words, Sanjit was crestfallen. It was his mother speaking and he felt helpless. All his life, the twenty-year-old had given into the wants of his parents like it was the law. But this time, he knew it would have to be different. This time he would have to follow the calling of his heart. Sanjit had come to realize it so unexpectedly. And once that happened, he knew that his life was never going to be the same again. He had tried to explain why he wanted to walk this path. But she had refused to understand, so there was nothing to do but disobey her.

But how could she agree with what her son had just proposed? There were other ways to doing what he wanted to do. In fact, after he finished his college, he was to begin a career in the Civil or Diplomatic services. He could live comfortably and still work for the betterment of society. He just had to walk the path laid out for him; a tried-and-tested way to success and happiness. Then how on earth had he got this silly idea in his head? If she let him go ahead with it, he would bring ruin upon himself and shame on the family.

The day Sanjit decided to move to a village, to dedicate his life to improving the lives of the poor, his mother stopped speaking to him. And it would be a full two years before she would come around to forgiving him.

Little did she know her younger son was going to make a big difference in the world. Time magazine, the prestigious American publication would call him one of the 100 most influential people in the world. He would also be named one of the 50 environmentalists who could save the world. That Sanjit would leave his home to become a hero for many.

Sanjit left quietly while the family disagreed with his decision and his mother cried silent tears. The year was 1967. The twenty-year-old had no idea what he was going to do. He just knew that he had to make the kind of impact that could benefit the life of others. He would not be able to live a life of luxury and the privilege it afforded after everything he had seen.

He boarded a train from the bustling town of Burnpur in West Bengal for a remote village in Rajasthan called Tilonia. As the steam engine chugged along taking Sanjit to his destination, he wondered how things had come to this. It was rare to feel dissatisfied despite having all that he had been blessed with.

When Sanjit was born in 1945, there was much rejoicing in the family. The second son, he was nicknamed 'Bunker', in keeping with the Bengali habit of giving rhyming names to siblings. His older brother was Shanker. The two boys together would run around the home all day, causing much mischief and mayhem. Their mother loved it. Shanker and Bunker were raised with love and abundant care in an affluent family. It was only natural that they received the best education too.

As he came of age, Sanjit was admitted into the Doon School at Dehradun. This was the place where the most elite children from all over India were sent to study. Famous for giving the country some of the finest politicians, actors, businessmen, the school had a stellar reputation for accepting and sending out the best into the world. By the time Sanjit had passed out from school, he already inhabited a rare world of achievers. He got admission for higher studies in St. Stephens College, Delhi. He was on the right track; any institution would be willing to accept him after college.

For Sanjit, life was a mix of his friends' company, keeping up with studies and lots of sports. Sanjit was particularly good at squash. Good enough to not only play as a national squash champion but also represent India in three world squash championships. All this while making sure his grades were top-notch.

Things would have gone as per plan had it not been for an unexpected trip to Bihar. In 1966–67, a terrible famine ravaged the state of Bihar. People were dying in thousands from the lack of food. When a lot of Sanjit's friends expressed their intention of going there and helping out in whichever way they could, Sanjit decided to go along too. Once there, he saw for the very first time in his life what hunger could do to humans. The stench of death and sickness was at close quarters. He realized how just one meal could mean the difference between life and death; that the value of a single effort, however small, could mean the world to someone in need. Along with his friends, he worked tirelessly till it was time to get back to college.

It became a turning point in his life. It made him question everything. His money, his education, the entirety of his world that now seemed to be enclosed in a bubble. His own problems—'Would he win his next squash competition? Would he excel at school? Could he get the job he was after?'—seemed so trivial and petty. It struck him like an epiphany, the truth about his education. He had been taught things about the world, but nothing about the ways one could change its sad realities. People were starving to death. And in no way could his exam results ever do anything to solve this problem. Wasn't his education pointless then?

Once back in Delhi, Sanjit knew he could never be the same again. He kept asking himself how his education could benefit that hungry, homeless woman in the village with three more mouths to feed. Or the man who had lost his legs and wanted to provide a dignified life to his children. Or maybe even the thousands of slum dwellers in the city who lived in cramped, closed spaces. Sadly, every time he came up with a blank.

What really agitated Sanjit was that with the passing of time, his questions were only multiplying while the answers proved just as elusive. Most people he spoke to looked down on living in the villages or working for the poor. Sanjit did not blame them. The formal education system imparted nothing to inculcate empathy for the helpless sections of society. Nor did it influence any desire in people to strive towards solving societal issues. Education was meant to equip them to make a life in glittering cities. Naturally no one would think beyond themselves and go live in primitive villages where even running water was a luxury.

Does he have a solution then? He had been asked this a million times. He did not. And that is why, as he looked out of the train window and watched the land change from lush green to the scraggy, dry, scorched earth of Rajasthan, he felt hopeful. Maybe, just maybe he could find some answers here.

To call Tilonia primitive would be an understatement. The village was dealing with acute water shortage. There was no electricity and telephones were an extravagance afforded to a select few, mainly the city dwellers. Roads were non-existent. But even if they had existed, Sanjit would not have known where to go. But he slowly started on the one thing that seemed the most necessary to him. Seeing how the paucity of water affected every aspect of the lives of the people, Sanjit began to work at digging wells for the village. This was easier said than done. The landscape of Tilonia was basically made up of infertile, desert land that had saline salt. Not only did that make growing anything difficult, it also made finding water a tough task. For an unskilled labourer like Sanjit, there was a lot of learning to do. Besides, the people of Tilonia looked at him with suspicion. They could not imagine why a young man, educated and so urbane had decided to land up in Tilonia. Something was definitely wrong with him and they were wary of him.

Day in and day out Sanjit would join the ranks of the poor, unclothed villagers in the sun, blasting wells till he could barely stand in the evening. But he felt alive in a way he had never felt before. His real learning had just begun. In the evenings, when the village elders sat together, he would watch them from a distance wondering how he could get to know them better.

Soon Sanjit joined the Catholic Relief Services to dig more wells in the village. And then when he saw the work that the Rajasthan Emergency Water and Agriculture Development Society (REWARDS) was doing to help create more water resources for the villagers, Sanjit knew this was what he wanted to do for the rest of his life.

The villagers had expected this strange young man to disappear in a few days. When that did not happen and they still saw Sanjit hanging around weeks after his arrival, they grew suspicious. "Are you on the run from the police? Have you broken the law?" the question addressed to Sanjit, startled him. The villagers were seated around a tree one cold evening, the crackling of the bonfire lit before them was the only thing to break the silence that followed the question. Sanjit who stood in the corner gathered the courage to walk tentatively towards the group.

As he approached them, more questions were directed at him, "Have you done something wrong? Or did you fail an exam and are staying here till your family calls you back?" asked another old man. An elderly woman joined in now as she asked him if he needed a government job and therefore was working in the village for a while. What they all wanted to know was what was wrong with him. Because any sane, educated man would come to the village only if he was banished or punished.

Sanjit now understood why he had been regarded with suspicion all this while. It was sad that a person like him was a rare sight to this village. Once again, he wondered if the education system was causing more harm than good. He smiled as he walked closer to them and replied that he was neither a fugitive from the law nor looking for a recommendation. "I have come here to help," he said simply. His words were met with silence and some disbelief. The villagers had never seen someone like him. But now that they had, they welcomed him into their fold. From that day on, Sanjit was accepted. It was the beginning of a new family even as he terribly missed the one back home.

As he got more access into the lives of the villagers, he observed that the real problems of the village would not get solved just by providing them water. There was far more to be done. The villagers needed to learn more modern techniques of cultivating the land. They needed access to better health care that could reduce the mortality rate of women and children. If this wasn't done, the development the government hoped for could only reach a limited, superficial point. These were his observations as an outsider.

As an insider, the more Sanjit lived with them, the more he learnt about their ways. All day he would work side-by-side with the villagers, picking up the techniques they used to find water and blast the wells. At night, by the fireside, he heard stories of their traditional knowledge and ancient practical wisdom passed down through generations. This was a whole new world opening up to him, a world that his school or university had never shown him. Sanjit was fascinated.

He met with unusual people that amazed him with their abilities. There were the water diviners, people who could accurately predict where water, a priceless commodity in the arid land of Tilonia, could be found. He saw how the village bone-setters could fix any broken bone with just the knowledge that was passed down to them. He heard the stories of the midwives in the village who could handle almost any kind of emergency during childbirth in the villages. These people astounded Sanjit. They were handling real challenges as best as they could, despite all the odds. Their ways were not primitive, in fact far from it. Their knowledge was not inessential, it was smart and creative. Sanjit was realizing that their way of life needed to not just be preserved but also encouraged and expanded.

For five years, Sanjit blasted wells in villages around Ajmer district. The more he interacted with villagers; the more he realized he wanted to start a college for them that could train them in providing solutions to rural problems. The villagers needed to get empowered to deal with their problems so that the thousands who left villages to live dark and depressing lives in the dirty slums of cities would choose to stay back.

With this mission clear in mind, Sanjit now began to conduct a kind of survey in over hundred drought affected areas to get a better idea of what the people needed. He even had a name in mind, 'The Barefoot College', chosen after the thousands of people who walked barefoot because they were too poor to own shoes. As the idea grew in his head, a sense of excitement came over him. The idea of the college was to ensure the people in the village became self-sufficient.

The way Sanjit saw it this was also a way to automatically address the other huge problem of the villager's migration to cities. The vast masses of people who migrated to live in the slums of big cities would never leave if they could work in the village with dignity; have access to clean drinking water and their children could get a decent education. He knew that this was the right way to go.

In order to kick-start the project, Sanjit began to travel around the country. He approached voluntary agencies in different states and studied the work they were doing, found solutions to his doubts and moved on to the next organization. He spent a year and a half doing this to prevent hiccups once the college began.

In 1972, at the age of 26, Sanjit established the Social Work and Research Centre (SWRC) in Tilonia. Also called the Barefoot College, it was not made to educate the villagers, for they already had abundant knowledge. It was rather an effort to help the 1,600 people of Tilonia, one of the eight Panchayat Samitis of Ajmer, to become self-reliant. Spread over an area of eight acres, the college was truly made for and by the people of Tilonia.

The project that had begun to solve the water crises in the village soon branched into a health and education program in a couple of years. By 1975, Sanjit managed to invite two young and very motivated women from the Tata Institute of Social Sciences (TISS) to join the Barefoot College as part of the teaching staff. Young and old, men and women were now being handed the key to a better life that they could lead in their own home.

But it wasn't just the older people; Sanjit wanted to include the most important and vulnerable part of the village population—the children too. About 60% of India's children do not go to school even today. A big reason for the problem is that children are expected to do household chores and help their families during the day. This was a unique problem particular to India and it required a uniquely Indian solution too.

Normally, school functions during the day because they are the preferred working hours for the staff. Sanjit began to envision a concept of a night school in Tilonia that would function as per the convenience of the children rather than the teachers. Since all day the children of the village worked at home, the night time would be perfect for them to come to school and study. He wanted to include practical knowledge in the curriculum so that it would help the children in their daily lives.

Therefore, in 1975, the first night schools of Tilonia were opened. At its forefront were placed the needs of the students. Hands-on learning was given to the children along with practical knowledge such as how to manage money or care for sick animals. Crèches for infants were also begun so that parents of the young could also have the chance to learn.

Early on, Sanjit had taken the decision to never award paper certificates to anyone who passed out from the Barefoot Institutions. Whether the person passing out was qualified or not was left for the community to decide, for whose sake and by whose efforts the college was founded.

Amidst the increasing numbers of students at the college, however, there was a set pattern Sanjit observed. The men came in large numbers while the participation of women was just as low. Yet, without exception it was the women who proved to be good students. They took their learning seriously and genuinely worked for the village betterment once they passed out of college. The men on the other hand were a restless lot. The moment they were done with vocational training of some sort, they would get themselves a job in the city and leave. This was defeating the very purpose with which the college had been established. Sanjit wanted these men and women to remain in the village and work for their own people.

After ruminating on the issue for long, Sanjit decided it was better to train women who were mothers and grandmothers! They had the patience to listen and learn slowly. They took the task assigned to them seriously and performed it with sincerity. Even though men and women both arrived with no background in education, there was a vast difference in what they gained in the college in six months. Sanjit saw how the trained women stayed within their communities and made positive contributions to the general welfare of their villages. He had finally found the students the country needed.

In the year 1984, Sanjit was honoured by being inducted in the Planning Commission of India. He was tasked with writing the policy statement of the 7th five-year plan. Without mincing words, Sanjit stood by his belief when he proposed that government money belonged to the people and every civil society must have access to it. For the first time in the history of India, an amount to the tune of one hundred and fifty crore rupees was set aside for the use of civil society groups. It was a step that shook the Indian Non-Government Organizations into action.

It was now time for a big step in the great wave of change that Sanjit was heading. He began by introducing the concept of solar lighting in the Barefoot College. By 1989, through sheer force of will, he had managed to make Barefoot College, Tilonia the only fully solar electrified college in Rajasthan. And by 2003, Sanjit had decided to train uneducated, rural women in as solar engineers. The decision was met with skepticism by many. It was not an easy task by any standards.

The donors doubted if the women would be able to do justice to the knowledge, time and money spent on them. The policy makers in the government too were doubtful if the women would make for efficient solar engineers. The husbands of these women worried that their wives would gain confidence to not put up with the traditional expectations and abuse which entailed their daily lives.

If anything, their doubts convinced Sanjit he was on the right track. Slowly and steadily women along with men were introduced into the course and taught to become solar engineers within six months. They came from remote villages. They came from all castes and religions. And at the College they were trained at their own pace so that they could go back to their communities and put their skills to use. He showed to everyone with example that middle-aged women could be trained. They were taught how to assemble, install, repair and maintain solar lights. They went and solar-electrified their own villages, places that had not seen electricity in a lifetime were now being lit up for the first time.

It was a game changer. A step towards empowering women was transforming entire villages. That was the strength of Barefoot College.

Areas that had no access to good schools or colleges, were now nurturing both young and old people to become solar engineers, teachers, accountants, doctors, computer instructors, midwives, carpenters, dentists, blacksmiths, solar cooker engineers, water testers and so much more. There was no profession that stood more respectable than the other. Everything was knowledge, everything was useful. These people were able to go back to their villages and serve them, thereby earning a respectable living as well as improving the lives of thousands. Migration to cities was slowly reducing. This milestone was what Sanjit had dreamt of all along.

Curiosity about his work was spreading and soon Sanjit was approached by international NGOs to train women of other countries. As an experiment, Sanjit decided to go to the remote villages of Afghanistan. There he observed the women to choose his potential students. Since he did not speak their language, he picked the students based on how much they valued the community and how they interacted with others. He then chose three women he thought could be trained as solar engineers.

The women lived primitive lives in small villages. Their husbands expected them to take care of their children and homes. They didn't even step out in the village much, going to another country seemed impossible. And the thought of becoming a solar engineer was beyond their imagination!

Sanjit and the organization that had invited him to Afghanistan managed to convince the women that they would be able to do it. Since their husbands did not want them to go on their own, Sanjit agreed to take their husbands and young infants along. Unsure of themselves, the women and their families arrived in Tilonia.

The first few days were alienating for them; from the food to the language to the clothes and especially the studies. But the staff at Barefoot College was extremely accommodating. They taught them solar engineering through a mix of sound, sight and gestures. For six months the three women learnt the intricacies of setting up and maintaining solar lamps. They were made to memorize the permutations and combinations of which wire would go where, through different colour codes—a technique developed by the College. The fact that they had to go back home and do this for their villages fuelled their courage. The college was good on its word and by the end of six months the entire village of Tilonia judged that the three women were now qualified to bring light into their communities.

The Government of India had agreed to pay the airfare for all such undertakings as well as the six-month education cost including food and stay. Various philanthropic organisations in Holland and America came on board to provide the hardware and bear the cost of the solar lanterns. Sanjit knew now that light was beginning to spread around the world.

These three women soon went back to Afghanistan, equipped with 150 solar panels from the Barefoot College. Once back, they did not just electrify their own homes, but their entire village. As per Sanjit's estimates, the cost of buying those 150 panels, insuring, transporting and installing them had been equivalent to the cost of 1 United Nations Consultant sitting in Kabul for a year. The only difference between the Consultant and the College was that the College's impact was visible and enlightening—quite literally!

Of the original team that had come to India, one woman then went back to Afghanistan to work with her grandson in installing the Reverse Osmosis Desalination plants. This plant makes it possible to remove the excessive salt from water to make it usable by the population. Afghanistan, destroyed by centuries of repression, was lit with knowledge and its power. In the village the solar engineers, the men would often sit around a bonfire in the evenings and women were not allowed to sit with them. One evening however, one of the solar engineers came to the bonfire and sat down with the men. There was much furor and the men naturally objected to her presence. She replied with confidence that now she was an engineer who had just as much right to sit there with the men. And nobody could argue with her on that.

The three women went on to train 27 more. Together, they for the first time brought light into a hundred villages in Afghanistan. Thousands were benefitted by a single act. A fifty-year-old woman from the village of Fariyad, who is one such solar engineer, set even higher standards. By 2005, she had single-handedly managed to electrify 200 houses. When the Afghani government arranged a tour of the village for the colleges of young engineers from the cities, the old lady confidently faced them, answering all the queries they had. She even explained to one Head of Department, the difference between Direct Current (DC) and Alternate Current (AC) since he didn't know it!

Meanwhile in India, Barefoot engineers were solar electrifying villages across the land. Over one hundred thirty-six inaccessible Himalayan villages were lit up. More than 23 villages across thirteen states in India began to develop the concept of the Barefoot College where independent centres were established.

Students began to come to the College from different parts of the globe. Till date, more than twenty Third World countries have benefitted from it. These were women from remote corners of the world, places where electricity was a distant dream. They were getting a chance to change their destinies, and that of their villages. And they were grabbing that chance with fierce force.

As far as the Barefoot College night schools were concerned, they too were doing their utmost. By the year 2000, Sanjit decided that like the College, even the schools must now be monitored and run by the children. More than seven thousand children went to cast their ballot and chose a candidate as Prime Minister and other Cabinet Ministers. The young girl who was elected to the post of the Prime Minister was a twelve-year-old who helped her mother cook and keep home, managed twenty goats during the day and helped with other household duties. At night she was a student, and along with her cabinet of twenty young boys and girls would take decisions on important issues such as education, empowerment, energy and women's issues related to the school.

Eventually, the young PM of the Barefoot Night School was chosen to receive the World's Children Prize for the Rights of the Child by an organization based in Sweden. When this young child, who had barely left her village, arrived in a foreign land, she was unfazed by the razzle-dazzle of the big city. Her poise impressed even the Queen of Sweden who asked Sanjit where this child got her confidence from. When Sanjit translated the question for the girl, she looked the Queen straight in the eye and said, "Please tell her that I too am the PM!"

The night schools in Tilonia have taught over fifty thousand children and most of them have ended up staying in the villages, immensely contributing in making the lives of the people better.

The dream that had begun with the decision to disobey one of the most important people in his life had now helmed a revolution of change. Sanjit's mother saw how her little boy had become the source of hope to so many. She spent the rest of her life blessing Sanjit for everything he had selflessly done for other people, and so he may continue to do so!

Acknowledgements

Gajra, the debt of gratitude I owe to you is so extraordinary that a 'thank you' couldn't even begin to describe it. But well, it's a start!

Shantanu, without the belief that you had in me I wouldn't have even begun this book. A big shout out to you! And also, a special thanks to Om Books International for publishing this book.

Chakrika, without you being by my side on this project, this book probably would not have seen the light of the day.

Michael J. Fox said, "Family is not an important thing, it's everything!" His words echo my feelings exactly. Without them, I wouldn't even be here! And what can be better than friends who are family too. I love you guys and you know who you are. (Yes, Ashumi. I have finally mentioned your name!)

I also want to express my gratitude to all the people who I have covered in this book. Thank you so much for 'being' there.

Bibliography

Borah, Prabalika. "Jadav Payeng Tells His Story as the Forest Man of India." *The Hindu*, December 2, 2020.

Bullock, Andrew. "Pride and Prejudice: Indian Royal Manvendra Singh Gohil on Being the World's First Openly Gay Prince." *Tatler*, June 20, 2022.

Captain Fantastic . FIFA+ Original Production, 2022.

CBC Radio. "Banned from the ring, bearded Sikh boxer fights religious discrimination." *CBC*, March 19, 2016.

"Chewang Norphel: The "Ice-Man" From Ladakh." *Milaap*.

Dixit, Kushagra. "Chewang Norphel: How a 'crazy' engineer solved Ladakh's water crisis." *The Economic Times*, March 12, 2018.

D'Souza, Shanthie Mariet. "Mumbai terrorist attacks of 2008." *Encyclopaedia Britannica.*

Dyu, Lily. "Chewang Norphel, the Iceman of Ladakh." *Climate Heroes.*

Films Division. "Pandit Bhimsen Joshi." YouTube, July 2, 2013.

Gandhi, Gopalkrishna. "An extraordinary existence." *The Hindu,* February 16, 2013.

"A Glimpse into the Life of Sardar Patel." *National Virtual Library of India*, 2016.

The Green Interview. "Bunker Roy – The Sage of Barefoot College." YouTube, July 27, 2022.

Grewal, Naina. "Boxing Beyond the Ring: Pardeep Singh Nagra." *Darpan,* January 31, 2019.

"Independence Day 2021: How Did Sardar Vallabhbhai Patel Integrate the Princely States? Check Details Here." *Firstpost*, August 13, 2021.

Jain, Aparna. *Boys will be boys: Inspiring stories for smart kids.* Context, an imprint of Westland Publications Private Limited, 2019.

Jamnalal Bajaj Foundation. "Shocked By Famine, This Inspiring Hero Transformed Villages Across Ten States." *The Better India*, July 10, 2018.

Kaudinya, Narayan. "Bateshwar Temples from the Eyes of the Legendary Archaeologist KK Muhammad." *Road to Nara* (blog), August 3, 2020.

Karan, Rewati. "Have to go beyond 377: After 9 years of marriage, India's 1st gay prince says fight not over." *ThePrint*, August 8, 2018.

Khurana, Suanshu. "Centenary: The Making of Pandit Bhimsen Joshi." *The Indian Express,* April 15, 2022.

Kumar, Anuj. "Certification doesn't establish competence: Sanjit Roy." *The Hindu*, March 26, 2022.

Latheef Naha, Abdul. "Major brings defence personnel together." *The Hindu*, June 03, 2022.

Madhav, Ram Madhav. "Sardar Patel and the Kashmir Question, Writes Ram Madhav." *Hindustan Times*, October 30, 2020.

Madhya Pradesh Tourism. "Bateshwar Temples of Madhya Pradesh – a Stupendous Feat of Restoration." *PR Newswire*, September 30, 2020.

"Major Sandeep Unnikrishnan: A Ten-Year Anniversary of the Mumbai Terror Attacks 26/11 Stories of Strength Book Extract." *Reader's Digest*, November 28, 2018.

McCarthy, Julie. "A Lifetime of Planting Trees on a Remote River Island: Meet India's Forest Man." *NPR*, December 26, 2017.

McMaster, William D., director. *Forest Man*. Polygon Window Productions, 2013.

Mehrotra, Puja. "Sam Manekshaw Was Key Architect of 1971 Win, but It Wasn't His Personal Success: Daughter Maja." *The Print*, December 17, 2021.

Milnes, Anthea. "Bunker Roy." *My Hero,* January 4, 2017.

Mysimran.info. "Interview with Pardeep Singh Nagra: Winning inside and outside of the ring." YouTube, November 27, 2018.

Nath, Hemanta Kumar. "India's 'Forest Man' Jadav Payeng Is on a New Mission to Make Mexico Greener." *India Today*, June 9, 2021.

"'Netaji' Subhas Chandra Bose: 9 things you didn't know about the inspirational figure." *India Today*, January 29, 2018.

Netflix India. "Remembering Major Sandeep Unnikrishnan." YouTube, July 14, 2022.

"Pardeep Singh Nagra." Pardeep Singh Nagra (website), 2018.

Pattanshetti, Girish. "From a small-town boy to Bharat Ratna." *The Hindu,* February 3, 2022.

Roy, Bunker. "Learning from a barefoot movement." TEDGlobal, July 2011.

"Remembering Sam Manekshaw: First Indian Army Officer to Be Promoted to Field Marshal." *CNBC TV18*, June 27, 2022.

Sahai, Shrinkhla. "Pt. Bhimsen Joshi: The making of a maestro." *The Hindu*, November 11, 2021.

"Sam Manekshaw: The Gentleman Soldier." *One India*, December 16, 2022.

Sangam Talks. "Story of Resurrection of 'Bateshwar' Group Of Temples." YouTube, May 3, 2018.

Shah, Javeed. "The Iceman of Ladakh: How Chewang Norphel's 'artificial glaciers' improved the region's water woes." *Firstpost,* August 12, 2017.

Singh, Major General Vinay Kumar. "Sam Manekshaw: The Gentleman Soldier." *India Today*, June 24, 2022.

"Sunil Chhetri Reveals What Prompted Him to Shoot Video for Football Fans." *DNA India*, June 3, 2018.

Tedx Talks. "Importance of Decriminalizing Homosexuality." YouTube, September 4, 2019.

Tripathi, Shailaja. "The Temple Guardian." *The Hindu*, February 10, 2013.

Vivek Bindra. "Subhas Chandra Bose." YouTube, January 23, 2021.

"What 'Major' Did Not Reveal: Major Sandeep Was Hugely Popular Among Girls!" *Outlook,* June 17, 2022.

Wikipedia contributors. "Vallabhbhai Patel." *Wikipedia*, January 24, 2024.

Zeidan, Adam. "Subhash Chandra Bose." *Encyclopaedia Britannica.*

"5 things about life and times of Subhas Chandra Bose." *Indian Express,* September 8, 2022.